Someone To Watch Over Me

Jerrie Alexander

Published by Alexander Publishing, 2024.

SOMEONE TO WATCH OVER ME

First edition. May 19, 2024.

Copyright © 2024 Jerrie Alexander.

ISBN: 979-8227889362

Written by Jerrie Alexander.

Chapter One

Stacey McKinney slid back the curtain a fraction of an inch and peered out. She squinted at the Texas sun bearing down. Billowy white clouds floated across a powder blue sky. Light flooded her room but not her heart.

She'd slept in spurts. Nightmares about men with knives and the sound of imagined footsteps had kept her awake. The result had left her with a splitting headache.

She washed down a couple of Advil with a cup of coffee, a trick she'd picked up from her dad, and tried to shake off the sense of foreboding that plagued her. As was her daily routine, she walked to the overly large front window and opened the blinds. Standing to the side, she thoroughly scanned the apartment complex grounds and parking lot. Seeing nothing suspicious, the muscles in her neck and shoulders slowly relaxed.

She closed the blinds, pushing bad memories to the back of her mind. She wasn't in Houston and nobody knew where she'd gone. It was time to focus on solving her immediate problem, the lack of money.

Working a second job to supplement her income wasn't the end of the world. It was a necessity. No way was she asking her father for funds. He'd help financially, but he'd be full of questions. Right now, she didn't have answers.

Moving back to Oak Hill had presented more than financial problems. Coming home had dredged up memories of an old heartache best forgotten. The image of Cash Butler's broad shoulders and turbulent gray eyes still haunted her. It wasn't a surprise when her heart fluttered over the news he'd moved back to town. Last she'd heard he'd been off in some foreign country saving America from terrorists. Where he lived meant nothing to her.

In times of need, people returned to their roots. She'd come home, where she intended to stay.

The Rockin' Boot, one of the town's popular nightclubs, didn't open for business until noon so she straightened up her tiny apartment and mentally rehearsed her interview. She'd heard they needed a weekend bartender, and she planned to be there to apply when the doors opened.

Stacey took meticulous care with her makeup and hair. A pair of jeans, a bright turquoise blouse, and her eel-skin boots finished the look. At a quarter to noon, she headed for the bar.

With the parking lot almost empty, she had no trouble finding a spot up close. She took one last look in the mirror. No matter how much Take-Me-Tonight lipstick she applied or how many times she fluffed her newly colored honey-toned hair, her nerve endings weren't going to stop sizzling until she at least tried to get this job. The worst that could happen was she didn't get hired and wound up working at the Whataburger on Main Street.

She'd driven past the Rockin' Boot last night and based on the number of vehicles there, the oversized dance floor still drew a crowd. The huge gun-metal gray structure hadn't changed much. The giant neon boot on top of the building was the same.

Without experience, she feared she'd have to do some convincing, but this was important. Wiping her sweaty palms on her jeans, she gathered her courage and opened the door.

The sounds of country music and the smell of stale beer assaulted her senses.

She could do this.

Within minutes, a waitress had escorted Stacey to an office in the back with instructions to wait for the owner. Unable to sit still, she wandered around the room, studying autographed pictures on the wall. A few of the visiting bands and singers had gone on to become famous.

"Stacey?"

Startled, she whirled at the sound of the familiar voice. Over the years, Brady Campbell had added a few pounds, but he was still an imposing figure. He reached out and clasped her hand.

"You remember me?" She liked his firm handshake. The steadiness of it helped calm her.

"Of course. You're Russell McKinney's daughter." His eyes widened, and he openly stared. "Except all grown up."

"Yes, sir." Stacey took the chair he pointed to and waited. Had changing her hair color from light brown to blonde caused such a look of surprise?

"I understand you're here about the weekend job." He sat and then propped his boots on the corner of his desk.

"That's correct." She kept her tone positive but upbeat.

"I'm puzzled as to why a woman with your means would want to work here." His forehead wrinkled, and his eyebrows drew together.

"If you're referring to my father's money, I'm too old to let him support me." Stacey felt the opportunity slipping away. That couldn't happen. She'd spent most of her savings on furniture and rent, leaving only the salary from her part-time job to pay the bills.

"I like your independence." He nodded as he spoke.

"How long you been back?" Brady was Texan through and through. His way of speaking made her feel at home.

"A few weeks."

"How's your dad?" Brady shoved his hand through his salt-and-pepper hair. Even under the bright lights in the office, judging his age was hard. He and her dad had been friends, but somehow Brady looked older. "He and his new bride moving home too?"

"No. They're living outside of Houston." She left out the exact location in case Brady developed the urge to contact her father. She had to keep her distance from her family until Ray Simmons got it through his thick skull that she wanted no part of him.

"What's he think about you being so far away?"

"It's only a few hours. Besides, I thought it best if I gave them some privacy."

"I hear you." Brady chuckled and dropped his feet to the floor. Leaning forward, he studied her for a long minute. "Let's walk and talk. You can convince me while I finish one last look-see before we get busy. All hell is about to break loose."

She followed him past the massive dance floor. She listened, trying to keep up and learn while they walked.

"How much bartending experience do you have?"

"Absolutely none." She laughed when his eyebrows shot straight upward. "I see nothing to be gained by lying to you and you firing me for it my first night. But I promise I'm a fast learner." She believed. Now to convince Brady.

"I respect your honesty."

"Good, because I wasn't joking, I need this job." She hadn't intended to sound so desperate or to cause the puzzled expression on his face.

"Take a left." He walked the length of the dance floor. "On the weekends we set up two beer stations. One on either side. Mixed drinks still come from the bar."

"Sounds like a good plan."

"It works. Part-time bartenders work Friday and Saturday nights from seven to closing. You're looking at three or four in the morning by the time your area is straightened and restocked. A barback will keep your beer tubs full throughout the night. Oh, and you'll share tips with him. Usually seventy-thirty."

"Did you just hire me?"

"I did. You want to start tonight or tomorrow?"

"Tonight." She jumped on it before he changed his mind.

"Then let's get your paperwork done. Be here an hour before your shift. I expect you to be on time. Take off only if you've covered your station with one of the other bartenders and cleared it with me."

"You won't have to worry about me not showing up."

"Good. Dress code is boots and jeans. Sexy is great for tips, but I remind all female new hires to use good judgment. I run a bar, not a strip joint." Brady scrubbed his hand over his chin. "I'll put Jonathan with you. His grandma passed some months back. He came home to put her affairs in order and decided to stay. He's a good worker. You'll catch on within the first few hours. The beer station is easy to master."

****

By nine o'clock Stacey's feet were killing her, and she was counting the hours until closing. "When did everybody stop aging at sixteen?" She joked with Jonathan, the bar-back, while they restocked the beer tubs.

"They might look young, but they're at least twenty-one," he said, his face solemn.

Did he think she was serious? "Lighten up, would you? I know the age requirement."

Jonathan's thin frame and pale blue eyes gave him a haunted look. He wore jeans, a red western shirt, and a red plaid bandana tied backward as if he were a highway bandit and might need to cover his face any minute.

Stacey liked him right away. It would be nice to have a friend. He'd jumped right in to help her learn the ropes, and they'd formed a good team.

He nodded at the counter behind her. "You got one waiting."

Stacey dried her hands and greeted the young cowboy leaning on the bar. "What can I get you?"

"Coors Lite, please, ma'am."

A spear shot through her heart. She turned to Jonathan, "Did he call me," she took a deep breath, "ma'am?"

"Sounded like it to me." He gave her a slight nod. Narrowing her gaze, she turned back to the baby cowboy. She crooked her finger, giving him the come here sign. Leaning over the bar, she met him nose-to-nose, and in a low growl, she repeated her question, "Did you call me ma'am?"

His lips spread into a beautiful smile. "Yes, ma'am, you heard me right. My mama always said I should be respectful of my..."

"Stop and think before you finish that sentence. You bring any ID with you?" There had to be a way to punish this young man.

"Always." He pulled his wallet from a hip pocket, produced a driver's license, and handed it over for her inspection.

She grinned at his birth date. Just as she expected, barely legal at twenty-two years old. She opened his beer and passed it and the license back to the young Adonis, feeling much older than the six years she had on him. Twenty-eight hadn't seemed old until she'd reported to work and got a look at the crowd. "Well, Lance—"

"You didn't let me finish. That's what my mama said. My daddy always told me, 'Son, find a beautiful older woman. She'll show you heaven here on earth.'" He gave Stacey a grin highlighted by a tiny dimple at the top right corner of his smile.

This young cowboy was a heartbreak waiting to happen but for someone other than her. Tall and lean with dark eyes, he couldn't have been out of braces long. He wore a bright blue button-down shirt and a summer silver-belly western hat.

"Does anybody ever stay mad at you?" She forgave his comment, but he'd struck a nerve. She was older than the other bartenders, and they had stayed busy all night. She'd have to get creative if she wanted to compete. Brady expected her to sell beer not chat with the occasional customer.

"Not for long. I'm interested in seeing heaven. Can I tempt you to show it to me?"

In her sexiest voice, she leaned over to him, "Sonny, your heart couldn't take the strain. Go away, you're holding up traffic."

****

Stacey dragged her tired butt out of the bar and into the sweltering heat. Summer in Texas was never timid, even at three forty-five in the morning. Soon the trees, grass, and lakes would be humbled by its power.

"Looks like you have company." Jonathan's voice had a touch of sarcasm in his tone.

"Lord, help me." She shook her head in surprise at the sight of the young cowboy leaning against a pickup. If Lance was anything, he was persistent.

"Interest you in a cup of coffee?" he asked, pushing off his hood and crowding into her space.

"Not even if you threw in pancakes." Her blood pressure spiked at the look of irritation that crossed the young cowboy's face. She pulled herself up to her full five-foot-eight. "I've been on my feet all night. I'm not going anywhere but home."

"What I had in mind didn't involve standing up." Lance winked, turned, and sauntered away.

"I don't like him," Jonathan muttered.

"He's a kid." Why she excused his behavior was a mystery. She got in her car and started it. "Jonathan?" she called after him. "Thanks for staying with me."

He raised his arm and wiggled his fingers without looking back. "No problem."

****

Saturday she went shopping and pulled out all the stops. She reported to work wearing a black-cropped tuxedo-cut western jacket over a white cami and black jeans. Her hair was down and, thanks to her curling iron, wavy.

Thankfully, her investment paid off, and the buzz at her station was instant. She was much busier than she'd expected. Halfway into the night, she'd emptied her tip jar, and much to her delight it was well on its way to being full again. Her feet were killing her, and her lower back ached, proving she'd been wrong to assume this job would be easy.

"Coors Lite, please, ma'am," the young man drawled heavily on the "ma'am."

Stacey looked up, already knowing that the beautiful baby cowboy had returned. Laughing at the bait, she opened a bottle and slid it across the bar to him.

"You didn't age much overnight," she wisecracked, and it felt good. For too long now, she'd looked over her shoulder, jumping at the sound of every male voice.

"Ahh, but you've lost a few years. Did you do all that for me?" His gaze hungrily took her in.

His flirting began to wear thin, but she laughed him off. "Please. I did it for tips. Check out the other bartenders. I gotta compete with them."

"I did, but I picked you. You're better looking without all the fixings." He leaned across the bar. "Have breakfast with me."

"Listen, Lance, you're barely past jailbait age, but you've got nerve. If I were ambitious enough to take on a younger man, you'd be my first choice. Thanks for the invitation, but I've sworn off men for a while."

"I'm not that much younger, you can't be over—" "I'm saving your life again, but this is the last time. Don't go around guessing a woman's age. If you go over, you can forget getting her into bed."

He smiled, showing his dimple. "I'll be around if you change your mind."

He walked away, leaving her in a great mood. His persistence gave her self-esteem a much-needed boost.

"Cute kid." Stacey couldn't help but smile.

"He's a bit stalkerish," Jonathan huffed. "If that's a word?"

"If it isn't, it should be."

Jonathan's response brought Ray Simmons and his threats slamming into her thoughts. Bad memories flipped her stomach upside down.

"It fits him," Jonathan muttered.

"Here they come." She indicated the customers leaving the dance floor.

"Always happens when the band takes a break."

The crowd kept them hopping, and the night flew past. She dipped a bar towel in a basin of water, and her bladder issued a warning not to be ignored.

"I'll be right back." Focused, she headed across the building on a mission. She skirted the two pool tables, moving faster the closer she got to the ladies' room door handle. A chill raced down her arms. She sensed someone moving in step directly behind her.

A scent stirred something in her memory. Awareness churned through her, warming her skin. Heat rushed to her lower belly. How did her body know to react? She turned to find Cash Butler smiling down at her from under the brim of his black hat.

"Would you look at who I found?" His whiskey-toned voice flowed over her skin like warm caramel over ice cream.

An old familiar zing of desire ricocheted through her nervous system. Twenty-eight was a good year for him. His black hair and stormy gray eyes still framed a chiseled jaw, sharp nose, and a mouth made to kiss. Ten years had added a maturity, a road warrior expression to his face.

First loves should never look this good. Never smell this good. And never stand this close.

He leaned down and buzzed his lips across her cheek, liquefying her knees. Blood coursed through her veins, revving her heart rate to racetrack speeds.

"Hey." Her attempt at sounding casual caught in the back of her throat. "Why aren't you off saving the world or fighting in the war or something?"

"Turns out I'm not bulletproof." His gaze raked over her, settling on her face. "You're looking well."

"So are you." She hated how her body reacted to his nearness. "I need to get back to work. So if you'll excuse me."

"Wait." He stepped between her and the door. "You're the reason I'm here tonight."

She pretended his strong hands sliding up and down her arms had no effect. Truth be told, seismic waves scorched their way to the ends of her fingertips.

"Unless you want your boots wet, you'll leave me alone."

"Then meet me at the Cactus Club tomorrow at two." One corner of his mouth lifted. "You remember how to get there?"

"Sunday is my day for scullery maid duties." Her brain issued a stern warning. His tone of voice said he was glad to see her, but his eyes gave nothing away. Meeting him wasn't a good idea. Unfortunately, her heart wasn't in the mood to listen.

"Since when do you do housework?"

"A lot's changed since..." She bit off the sentence. Confiding in Cash served no purpose.

Letting him touch her had been a mistake. Did she pull away? Nooo. She stood there while his hands traveled down until his fingers twined through hers.

"I'll be there tomorrow at two. I hope you'll come." Her bladder, which was soon to erupt like Mount Vesuvius, issued a final warning. Stacey nodded her agreement and rushed into the restroom. When she came out, Cash was nowhere to be seen. And she had no way to retract the date.

Her bar was stacked three deep when she returned, and Jonathan's expression of disapproval wiped Cash Butler from her thoughts. "Sorry."

"The crowd's killing me," he muttered, moving to the tubs of beer and turning his back to the bar.

They finished off the night, squared up her station, and counted out the tips. Jonathan pocketed his share and walked out with her.

Again after closing, the baby cowboy waited next to her car. She sent him on his way wondering how many times she'd said no to him tonight. At least he took her refusals like a gentleman. She thanked Jonathan for waiting and drove home.

Tired beyond imagination, she showered and went straight to bed where she stared at the ceiling. She tried to fall asleep, but Cash's appearance pulled on her emotions. Could they ever be just friends? She couldn't allow more. He'd hurt her badly once. She wouldn't allow it to happen again.

Even by the light of the pool tables, his smoky gray eyes had hinted at a hard edge to his personality. Had his time in the military left him harsh and bitter?

He'd grown up poor with no father and a mother who worked two jobs. Back then, Stacey hadn't agreed with his belief that love didn't last forever. Obviously, he'd meant it or he wouldn't have professed his undying love and then deserted her.

****

Stacey drove into the Cactus Club parking lot and killed the engine. Even during the daytime, neon lights blinked a frantic rhythm around the outline of a monster orange cactus. The building sat at the back of a huge parking lot, making the location the perfect place for a secret rendezvous. Which, she reminded herself, was not why she'd come.

She was still adjusting to the cave-like atmosphere when a pair of hands slid around her waist and snuggled her body against his. Instinctively, she breathed in his woodsy scent and leaned back against him. "I'd recognize that touch anywhere."

He laughed, and his chest rumbled against her. The sound was real and sincere. Controlling her emotions around him was going to be like treading water in a tidal wave.

"Sug." He breathed her old nickname into her hair. "It's good to hold you in my arms again."

He buried his face in her neck. His warm breath sent a flush up to her hairline. Stacey turned to face him. Her eyes feasted. Her skin heated. She might as well have been standing in the middle of a forest fire. *Back away from the flame.*

"It's been a long time." Stacey dragged her hormones under control. "Your self-confidence has improved in the past ten years."

"Age and the military taught me to reach out if I want something." He tilted his head, leaned in, and brushed her lips lightly with his. "I'm glad you're here."

Stacey breathed deeply trying to regain control over her hormones. She slipped her arm in his. "Lead on."

She followed him to a booth in the back corner of the building. The lights were dim but at least you could see the person across from you.

The desire to hear how life had treated him churned in her stomach. Had he ever been in love? Married? Missed her? His unreadable eyes gave nothing away.

"Last night you said you're not bulletproof. How badly were you hurt?"

"Took a bullet in the leg. Screwed up the bone." He shrugged. "No big deal."

He avoided her gaze, contradicting his statement. Having to leave the military was probably a really "big deal" to him. "I think maybe it was."

"The Army needs men who are a hundred-ten percent ready." He lifted one shoulder. "I'm a hundred."

"After all your world travels, what does Oak Hill have to offer you?"

"A lot, now that you're here. Want to tell me why you're back?"

Stacey's heart skipped a beat. Typical Cash, he went straight to the heart of the matter. He'd been her protector when they were kids, long before young love had complicated their lives. He'd watched over her, even protected her from a couple of schoolyard bullies who thought they could take her swing. Thinking back, she'd probably fallen for him then.

The need to touch him won. Reaching across the table, she took his hand. "I'm fine."

"You're lying, but I'll respect your privacy." Cash stroked her knuckles with his thumb, scorching her flesh. "For the time being."

Stacey smiled at his insinuation. "What? Are you going Billy-Bad-Ass on me again?" She leaned back and looked him over.

Cash coughed out a laugh, "Are you saying I was overprotective of you back when?"

"Not at all. After Mom died, Dad was always too busy. You were there for me."

His smile turned angelic. It gave him the look of elegance. His lips, full and tilted upward at the edges, accentuated a sensuous mouth and made him look as if he knew something no one else did. His movements were fluid and deliberate.

They'd never talked about her father's money or Cash's poverty. She'd blamed his financial situation for him surprising everyone by joining the Army. He'd broken her heart when he left without saying goodbye.

Funny, after all these years, just thinking about that time in her life still made her chest ache. Cash was all Texan—boots, black Wranglers, tailored white shirt, and always, no matter the season, a black felt western hat. He was a feast for the eyes, ramping up his sex appeal by looking down behind long black eyelashes.

"Do I pass inspection?" Leaning across the table, he whispered, "I can be had, you know. You keep looking at me like I'm the lunch special, I'll pay the tab, and we'll locate the closest mattress."

"Hmm, what a generous offer. As incredibly romantic as it sounds, I'll pass." They shared a laugh, and Stacey marveled at how easily she'd relaxed. "You didn't answer my question. This part of the country can't have much of an appeal to someone who's been all over the world. What's next?"

He stared at her hand in his, and a cold, viselike grip seized her heart. Was he leaving again?

"I bought a place outside of town. Nice spread for a horse ranch. Take a drive with me?"

She hesitated, trying to decide if accepting his invitation was a good idea.

"Come on. Leave your car here. I'll bring you back." He extended his hand. "Unharmed."

"I'll hold you to that."

Probably not a smart move, but she'd committed. He'd been wild and restless in his youth. Had age settled him down? *Not that it mattered.* A temporary relationship with him was like waving a red flag at an angry bull—a sure way to get trampled or gored.

He stood and helped her to her feet. They walked outside together. His hand rested on her lower back, making her knees weak.

Cash opened the pickup door for her, leaned across, and then fastened her seat belt. She wasn't helpless, but who was she to deny him the pleasure? She lowered her eyelids, allowing his scent to wrap around her. The fresh aroma of the woods, clean air, and sunshine turned her bones to jelly. Soft lips pressed against hers. She opened her eyes to find his face inches from hers. Storm clouds gathered behind his eyes.

"Uh-uh," she said despite wanting to lean in for another taste. "Not happening. I've sworn off men."

"All men?"

"Yes. You in particular."

"A challenge? We'll see if I can change your mind." He dragged a finger along her jawline, sending a shiver up her spine. "Besides, I couldn't help myself. It was too tempting."

Chapter Two

He'd lost his mind. Must have. Cash had no other excuse for pretending their prior relationship hadn't been a disaster. His Stacey, the fresh-faced girl with the innocent bloom of youth, had haunted his dreams many hot nights during his stint in the Army. This Stacey had grown into a stunningly beautiful woman.

Locating her had crossed his mind many times, but he'd figured she'd be caught up in the high-society life her father wanted for her. Dear Old Dad hadn't approved of the kid with holes in his jeans whose mama scrubbed toilets for a living.

Cash's belly rolled into a knot. Was taking Stacey to the ranch without telling her a mistake? How would she react? And why was it so damned important she be pleased? Better to warn her. He pulled the truck onto the gravel shoulder and stopped.

"I need to tell you..." He paused when her blue eyes reflected concern.

She touched his arm, sending napalm-like streaks straight to his groin. "There's nothing you can't tell me."

He stared, mesmerized for a second. *Oh, hell. Grow a pair and tell her.* "I bought your old home place."

She sat silently for the longest time. Cash tried to keep up with the myriad of changes that passed behind her gaze. He waited patiently, letting her sort through her feelings. He needed the truth, not a lie to placate him.

Unless she'd changed, she'd never been a good liar. It had been her honesty about the two of them that had resulted in a visit from her father and the sheriff. Looking back, Cash hated how he and his mother had allowed themselves to be bullied. He'd opted to join the Army to avoid a trumped up charge designed to send him to jail. Her dad had laid it out plain and simple. Cash Butler wasn't, and wouldn't ever be good enough for his baby.

"Are you happy living there?" The corners of her mouth lifted, but her expression shouted, *help me out here 'cause I'm at a loss for words*.

"I guess that's an honest first question." If only he had a good answer. "The place feels more like home now that the renovation is complete."

Now who was lying? He could've been honest and confessed he'd originally bought the ranch out of spite. A stupid effort to prove his worth. Thankfully, after the first horse was unloaded, he'd released those old resentments.

Or had he?

"Show me." Her tone sounded sincere, and the knot between Cash's shoulders relaxed a little.

Back out on the highway, he hooked a right and drove under the archway where the McKinney Angus Cattle Ranch sign had hung. He'd had it replaced with one that read, Butler Quarter Horse Ranch. If she had pangs of resentment, her face didn't show any signs.

"You graveled the road back to the house." Stacey rolled down the window, allowing her long blonde hair to billow around her shoulders.

"Not me. The family I bought the place from made some changes of their own. When the husband died, the wife wanted to move closer to relatives in San Antonio. I was in the right place at the right time."

He parked in front of the ranch house and hopped out to open Stacey's door. Her gaze scanned the area and then came to rest on his face. Chills raced up his spine. What was going through her mind? He hoped bringing her out here didn't dredge up sad memories.

"I'm glad you bought it. The place suits you." She stepped down and wrapped a strand of hair around her finger, a habit he remembered her having when they were teenagers. The familiarity of her action sent surges of undefined emotions racing through him.

What thoughts were running through her mind? Did coming here reopen the pain of losing her mother? Did Stacey remember Cash's declaration of undying love sitting right there on those steps? Or did she think about how her father made an impoverished, unworthy eighteen-year-old boy feel when he ran him out of town?

A lot of time had passed. Seeing her—being near her—sent ideas racing through his mind and made him wonder. Could a person ever really go home again? He'd walked away from her once and didn't think he could do it again. Things were different now. The poor kid from the wrong side of town didn't exist anymore. This grown man didn't scare and never ran from anyone.

"House or barns?" she asked.

"What?" He hated to ask her to repeat herself. Felt stupid for letting his thoughts wander.

"Where to first?"

"The barns. I want to introduce you to someone."

Stacey accepted his extended hand and followed him to what once had been a cattle barn. Inside, his chest swelled with pride when her face lit up at the changes.

Horse stalls lined the walls. A wash rack, tack room, and feed storage finished the transformation.

"I can see why we came here first," she said, sounding pleased. "This is impressive."

"I wanted you to see the changes, but there's more." He walked down the aisle, stopping outside a stall.

Stacey peeked over the gate. Her jaw dropped. She was staring at a magnificent sorrel foal, a colt. "He's beautiful." She glanced around. "Where's his mother?"

"She died two days after giving birth." He caught the shift in her eyes. Damn, he hadn't brought her out her to make her sad. "Luckily, he got that first mother's milk. It gave him a good beginning." Cash's throat tightened. A lot rode on this colt. The first offspring of his stallion, a good showing in the sale barn could establish the ranch's name. "One of the boys located a nurse mare. She'll be delivered today. If the foal won't nurse, we'll bottle-feed him every hour."

Stacey held out her hand, and the young horse backed away. "It's okay," she spoke in soothing tones. "You don't have to trust me."

Fearlessly, she opened the stall door and stepped inside, moving slowly. She stopped a foot away and held out her hand again. Cash's heart did a weird squeeze when the young stallion moved closer, allowing her to stroke his neck.

"He likes you." *So do I. And that could be a mistake*. The fact she hadn't answered his phone calls all those years ago still stung. That she'd bowed to her father's belief that Cash wasn't good enough for her shouldn't still eat at him, but it did. He shook off those thoughts. She was here and that's all that mattered.

Stacey stepped out of the stall into the aisle. She turned when the colt nickered, and she stumbled over a water hose. Cash reached to steady her, but she tumbled to the hard floor. Sweeping her into his arms, he carried her to a bale of hay.

"I'm fine. Put me down."

"You sure you're not hurt?" He sat her down and knelt in front of her. He brushed her cheek to inspect for bruises. Her eyes flashed wide, and her lips parted. Lush, pink, and moist, her mouth begged to be kissed. So he took off his hat, leaned in, and did exactly that.

****

Lightning bolts shot in every direction, mostly in the area of Stacey's lower belly. Cash's earlier kiss had been a beginning, an exploration. This was a full-out assault. Tossing resolve aside, she put both hands on the back of his head and pulled him to her. Her lips reacquainted themselves with his. The effect swept away all reason. His tongue painted exotic pictures of future delights. He wanted her. The evidence pressed hard against her leg.

Holy crap. She'd jumped on a runaway train. Her brain warned they were screaming downhill out of control, but her body begged for more. She shifted her position, allowing him to slide between her thighs, moaning when he rubbed against her.

A cease and desist signal kept circling, refusing to be ignored. Finally, with great effort, she pushed him away. She straightened her blouse and smoothed her hair. He tilted his head to one side, ran his thumb down her jaw, and then gently kissed her forehead.

"Look." Her ragged breathing made speaking difficult. "I can't explain what's happening. Maybe it's old memories. Maybe there's something real happening. I don't know if I can handle it right now."

There. She'd been honest. Could she trust that he wanted to recapture what they'd lost? His expression softened, and he looked her straight in the eyes.

"Then we take baby steps because what's happening is 'real.' But there's more going on here. What's got you so skittish? I can't lend a hand if you won't tell me."

"I don't need help."

"My gut tells me you're wrong." He sighed when she didn't speak. "Come on, I'll show you the stallion barn and the house."

The exterior grounds, with the new horse corral and hot-walker, bore little resemblance to when she'd called this place home. When they started toward the house, her heart stumbled. She half expected to see her mother step out and wave. Losing her to cancer had left twelve-year-old Stacey heartbroken.

Cash's arm rested on her shoulder. The smile he'd worn earlier had vanished. "I'm sorry," he said. "I should've realized. Let's get out of here."

She leaned against his muscular frame. With him supporting her, she could do this. "No. I want to go inside."

The walk up the path and through the gate was eerie and threw her a little off balance. Memories of how hard she'd fought against the move to Houston flooded her. In the dreams of her eighteen-year-old brain, she'd expected Cash to ride in on a white horse and save her. He hadn't.

"You sure?" Cash stood so close his warm breath caressed her skin.

"Yes." She straightened her shoulders and stepped through the door, hoping to embrace the place as his home.

The interior had taken on a distinctly masculine feel. Gone were the bright colors her mother had loved. Dark paneling covered the living room walls and hardwood floors displaying a collection of original Indian handmade throw rugs. The coffee table was one of those constructed out of a tree stump variety and had been varnished many times to produce a dazzling sheen. A mahogany leather couch and two overstuffed chairs flanked by small tables reflected Cash's taste.

A painting hung over the fireplace, an old cowboy sitting in front of a roaring fireplace, weather beaten boots by his chair, and a sleeping dog at his feet. The man appeared to be dozing with a dream overhead of a young man riding a wild bucking horse.

The house was all Cash. The tension between her shoulders eased. Her mother would've approved.

"How long have you been back?" Stacey asked, moving around the room, marveling at the changes.

"Almost two years."

"You've accomplished a lot in that length of time. The ranch looks great. How's your mother?"

"She passed away." He shook his head as if waving off sympathy. "A drunk driver ran a red light and T-boned her car. She suffered for a few months. Went to sleep one night and didn't wake up."

"I'm sorry. You were with her when she passed?" "Yeah. I barely made it home in time."

The sadness in his eyes sent Stacey searching for a new subject. She said the first thing she could think of. "You never married?"

"No. The woman I wanted...how about you?"

"Me? No way." Why hadn't he finished his sentence? Who was the woman? Stacey wanted to ask, but she wouldn't. "Never even close."

In ground-covering strides, Cash crossed the room and wrapped his fingers around her arms. His gaze locked on her, thunderclouds clashed behind his eyes.

"Why did you come home?"

"Maybe I came to see if you were here." She hadn't intended to say that, but he kept pushing her for a reason. Why was it so important to him? Even if she confided in him, he couldn't help.

"I don't think that's why."

Anger suddenly swamped her. Anger she didn't understand. "You're right. Why would I expect you to be in Oak Hill when you couldn't wait to leave?"

"What? I..." Judging by how fast he clamped his teeth closed, he wasn't sure what to say. She opened the front door and started to the wraparound porch.

"I'd like to go back to my car."

The ride back to the Cactus Club was awkward and silent. Her emotions were all over the place. One minute, she wanted to pull him close. To cling to him. To trust they could recapture the past. The next she wanted to lash out at him like a scorned teenager.

He parked, and they sat staring straight ahead for a minute.

She turned to face him. "Meeting you today was a mistake."

"I'm glad you did." His always unreadable eyes never flinched. Leaning toward her, he tucked a card in her purse. "My cell number."

Fighting the urge to tell him everything, she drove from the parking lot without glancing back.

A stop at the local big-box store and she'd bought more than enough food to last the week, along with a no-contract cell phone. Stacey loaded her groceries into the back seat of her car.

A sudden gust of wind hit her. The hair on the back of her neck rose. A shiver rushed up her spine. She whirled around expecting to find someone directly behind her, but found no one. She couldn't shake the feeling of eyes being trained on her.

Somebody was watching.

Chapter Three

Stacey looked forward to Friday night. The fast pace, loud music, and happy people helped her forget the constant feeling of being stalked. The steady flow of customers helped block out thoughts of Cash too. Most of the time. He didn't have her phone number or know where she lived, but the question nagged at her. Could it have been him at the grocery store? Had he followed her?

A cold hand wrapped around her arm and Stacey whirled around. Wide-eyed, Jonathan jerked back.

"Sorry." They both laughed off their overreaction. "You surprised me!"

"You couldn't have forgotten I was back here." He stacked the cold cases of beer on the counter and then began separating them into singles. "Who are you expecting?"

"Nobody," she lied.

"Liar. You've been looking over your shoulder all night."

"Really? I can't imagine why."

"Can I get a beer over here?" Cash's whiskey-toned voice washed across her.

God help her, she'd missed him. Missed his touch. Missed his kiss. Missed being near him. Plus, she had to ask if he'd been watching her. No doubt, he'd tell her the truth.

"Sorry, I don't recall your brand."

One corner of his sexy mouth lifted. "That would be Coors."

"Lite?"

"No thanks." His gaze dropped to her mouth. "I prefer mine full-flavored."

Her skin warmed from the inside out. Heat rushed up her cheeks. God. She was blushing like a school girl. How had Cash ordering a beer turned into a sexy exchange of words?

Jonathan cleared his throat and held an open can in front of her.

"Thanks," she mumbled, passing the beer to Cash.

"Thanks." His fingers covered hers on the cool can. "I hope a week without me was long enough."

She held up a finger indicating he should hang tight a minute. Her stomach roiled in turmoil while she waited on a couple of customers. One day without him had been too long, but she wasn't about to tell him.

The line at her station thinned, giving her a chance to talk with him. She leaned as close as possible. "Have you been following me?"

"Stalking isn't my style. I could've tracked you down, but wouldn't have won any points for it." His eyes narrowed to slits. "Why?"

Stacey lifted one shoulder. Maybe her imagination had gone completely haywire. Was she reinventing monsters from her past? Becoming paranoid for no reason? She had no proof Ray had tried to find her. If she were lucky, he'd forgotten she existed.

"A shrug isn't going to cut it. You don't ask a question like that without an explanation."

Stacey caught Brady out of the corner of her eye. Not a good thing to be caught paying attention to just one customer. "Go away. My boss is headed this way."

"I'm not leaving without your number."

She wrote her cell number on a bar napkin and then pushed it in front of him. "Now go. I have work to do."

"I'll call tomorrow." He touched the brim of his hat with his finger and then sauntered away, leaving his beer untouched.

She and Brady checked her backup stock. He always made sure she wouldn't run low. When the band took a break, her station would fill with customers.

"You made a new friend." Lance held up his beer bottle to indicate he wanted a refill.

"Not new. We grew up together."

"Should I be jealous?" Lance asked.

"What you 'should' do, is look elsewhere for a girlfriend." Stacey pushed his fresh beer down the bar to him and turned to the next customer.

The rest of the night flew by. The crowd ebbed and flowed with the band breaks. The traffic was enough that when Stacey took her swollen feet and aching back out to her car, home was all she could think about. The sight of Lance leaning against her car sent irritation shimmying up her spine.

"How about breakfast?"

Tired down to her toenails, she snapped, "I don't know how else to say this, so here goes. No date. No breakfast. Grow up and take no for an answer."

She unlocked her car and threw her purse across to the passenger side. She got in and slammed the door. Jonathan walked past and waved, but waited until she drove away.

Minutes later, a vehicle roared up behind her, its headlights almost blinding her. Her first thought was that she'd made Lance angry, but he was too good natured to be insulted by a rejection. Based on the angle of the glare ricocheting off her rearview mirror, she guessed it to be a car. It moved closer, so she sped up a little. But the car matched her speed. Then it slowed and turned down a side street.

What was that? Drunk driver? Her body shook, cold from the inside out.

Paranoia ate away at her resolve to be strong, so she drove through the apartment complex's parking lot twice, checking for any evidence of Ray or Ray's car. Because of him, she'd learned how easily a person could misinterpret an innocent customer service smile.

Finding nothing disturbing, she parked and went inside.

She opened the fridge and stared at the contents. Not hungry but needing to eat, she decided on cereal, snacking while she got ready for bed.

She hoped she'd made her point with Lance. Maybe now, he'd give her a wide berth from now on. The last thing she needed was trouble with him.

After a nice hot shower, Stacey crawled into bed. She stretched her legs and wiggled her toes, celebrating the removal of her tight jeans and boots.

****

Someone pounded on her front door, jolting her from a deep sleep. Panic seized Stacey's lungs, making breathing an effort. Other than her landlady and two bosses, no one knew how to find her. The loud racket started again, only this time, it sounded like the world was coming to an end.

Stuffing her feet into jeans and tugging a shirt over her sleep tee, she hurried to the door and peered through the peephole. A chill rushed across her arms and down her spine. Two cops standing outside the door at nine o'clock on a Sunday morning couldn't possibly be bringing good news. She pushed her hair off her face and opened the door.

"Stacey McKinney?"

"Yes. What's wrong?" Nerves knotted painfully in her neck.

The older man offered his ID. "I'm Sergeant Kelly. This is Officer Barnes. The owner of the Rockin' Boot provided us with a list of employee names."

She glanced up from his badge. "Something happened at the bar after I left?"

"May we come in?" The sergeant ran his hand down the front of a wrinkled white dress shirt.

"Of course." The circles under both men's eyes made her think they'd missed a lot more sleep than she had. She waved them inside and led them to her small kitchen table.

"You spoke with Lance Pierson last night?"

"Yes. A couple of times. He was walking toward his pickup the last time I saw him." She returned the detective's ID. "Why? What's he gotten himself into?"

"I'm sorry to tell you, he's dead." He pulled out the small kitchen chair, turned it backward, and sat. "You may have been one of the last people he spoke with."

"No," she insisted. "He was fine when I drove away." Stacey gripped the countertop to steady herself. "This can't be true."

"What can you tell us about the last time you saw the deceased?" Detective Kelly set a small recorder on her table and waved her to a chair. "Do you mind if record our conversation?"

The word 'deceased' sent shock waves rolling through her system. It was so final and cold. As if when a person died they ceased being a person and became a thing. Her heart raced, her stomach cramped, and her mother's death flooded her memory. She dragged her emotions inside and concentrated on helping the detective.

"Do you record all your interviews?"

"If I've been up all night, I usually do. It's just so I don't forget to write something down. You want it off?"

"No. It's fine. What happened?"

"The decease..."

"Stop it. He has a name. Lance. He's still Lance."

"Sorry. Mr. Pierson was found with his throat cut this morning."

Stacey couldn't process that statement. She must have misunderstood. "Excuse me?"

"He didn't report to work this morning. A coworker called and had the apartment manager check on him."

Tears sprung to her eyes. "He's just a kid."

"Was," the detective corrected her. "What can you remember about your last conversation with him?"

Stacey took a calming breath and then tried to remember every detail of her conversation with Lance in the parking lot. She struggled to control the quiver in her voice. "Do you have any suspects?"

"No one in particular. We can't rule anyone out just yet, but based on the extreme violence of the murder, my gut tells me a woman didn't kill Lance." Kelly's expression softened a little.

"Every possibility has to be considered, but this is all standard procedure. It would be helpful if you could verify what time you arrived home."

"The only person who could is the jerk who almost ran over me on the way home. Scared the crap out of me. But he turned a few seconds later. I figured it was a drunk driver." She hoped what she'd said was true.

"Can you describe the vehicle?"

"I think it was a car. All I saw was bright headlights barreling up behind me. If I had slowed down they would've rear-ended me." She wasn't going to mention Ray. Her gut reaction wasn't proof he was in town.

"If you remember anything about the vehicle, give me a call. Let's get back to your last conversation with Mr. Pierson."

"I will. Listen, Lance was a great kid. He was funny, flirty, and sweet. I can't imagine anyone wanting to harm him." Stacey's stomach rolled. "He regularly waited for me in the parking lot with an invitation for coffee, breakfast, or an overnight stay at his place. But the offer was done in a good-natured way."

"And that happened again last night?"

"Yes. I told him no and he left. I just can't imagine anyone wanting to harm him."

"Somebody did. And I intend to find out who." Kelly turned off the recorder, smiled, and then stood.

"I hope you do and he goes away forever."

He nodded and dropped his card on the table. "Remember to give me a call if you think of anything."

Stacey closed the door behind him and the officer. She touched her fingers to her neck. Anger welled up inside her. It was so unfair that someone would kill Lance. She wrapped her arms around her waist. What a horrible way to die.

She sunk onto the couch remembering his wisecracks, his quick smile, and his lust for life.

It took three tries to punch in Cash's number. She knew if she needed him, he'd be there. Her lips trembled so badly that the only word she could force out was his name.

"Cash." She stared at the phone wondering why she'd been compelled to dial his number.

"Sug? You okay?"

"The cops were just here." Her mouth moved but nothing else came out. Was she overreacting? Just because her stalker, Ray Simmons, had threatened to kill anyone she cared about didn't mean he'd found her. Nor did it mean he'd follow through on his threat just because Lance had been friendly. "Can you come over?"

"Tell me where."

Tears breached the surface and flowed down her cheeks. Somehow, she managed to rattle off her address.

"I'm on my way."

Knowing that Cash would be there soon helped calm her. He hadn't asked why she needed him. That she did, was all he needed to hear. His actions spoke volumes straight to her heart.

Stacey fixed a pot of coffee, watching the dark liquid drip into the carafe, as if staring would hurry the process along. She poured herself a cup before the liquid stopped dripping and carried it to the couch. She dragged a quilt up to her neck and curled up to wait.

Lance was all she could think about. His pretty face, his full-of-life personality, his gift of charm, all of those qualities had been lost forever.

Granted, she hadn't known him very well, but nobody deserved to die like that. His family would suffer the soul-numbing pain of losing a loved one. Just the way she had when her mother died.

A light tap on her front door had her kicking the guilt to the floor and getting to her feet.

"Stacey," Cash called out from the hallway.

"Coming." She opened the door and stepped into his arms. Here she felt safe and protected. He leaned his head back and gazed at her, brushing her eyes, cheeks, and lips, tracing the planes and valleys with his fingers.

"Who made you cry?"

"Come in. I'll tell you." She leaned into his palm when he cupped her cheek. "Thank you for coming."

"Anytime. Anywhere. What happened?"

Stacey led him to the couch and repeated her conversation with the police. The longer she talked the darker his eyes turned.

"I'm sorry you had to hear the news that way. So why were they questioning you?"

"Lance and I talked in the parking lot after I got off. According to the detective, I may have been the last person to see Lance alive."

"Not the last." Cash's tone was soft but firm. "The killer saw him after you left the parking lot. "Did he give you the impression he expected trouble?"

"No. On the contrary. He was upbeat. Full of life." Cash stood and paced. He crossed her small living room in a couple of strides. At six-foot-three, his broad shoulders, muscled arms, and narrow waist presented a remarkable sight. Something stirred inside her. Something deep. Something that made her want to tell him everything.

"Something is missing. What are you not telling me?"

If she told him about Ray could she be putting him in jeopardy?

"Come on, Sug. You can trust me? You know that, don't you?"

She nodded. "Of course. I hate to drag you into my past." She held up her hand to stop his protest. "Trouble may have followed me to town." The words were hard to say, and her voice was a whisper.

The dark clouds behind his eyes made her want those words back.

"What kind of trouble and what makes you think that?"

She shook her head. Stupid thing to say or think. Ray had no idea where she was hiding. "It's nothing."

"Nothing my ass. I see the fear in your eyes." Cash caught her chin with his thumb and forefinger, lifting it until her gaze met his. "Tell me."

She refused to deal with possibilities. Refused to believe Ray had found her. Refused to think about death and the young man it took.

"Kiss me," Stacey whispered. Cash could make her forget, if only for a minute.

One corner of his mouth lifted making her insides clench. He slid her hair back over her shoulders, took a handful, and pulled her head back. Her insides melted. She wanted to consume him, wanted to be consumed by him, to push death and fear from her mind.

His lips slid across her forehead down her nose and then gently covered her lips. Searching. Exploring. Slowly, he pulled away. He tenderly kissed her forehead and then lazily walked to the kitchen. He opened cabinet doors until he located one of the few cups she owned, which he filled with coffee before returning to the couch.

Why had he broken away? She wanted to forget for a few minutes, but he'd deliberately put distance between them.

"I've never made love to a woman that didn't want me to, and I'm not going to start today. You're upset and scared. It's not unusual. Sex is a perfect way to reaffirm life."

Stacey relaxed, realizing he was right. "When did you get so smart?"

"I know that this isn't what you want." He calmly sipped his coffee, watching her over the rim of his cup. "You ready to tell me what's troubling you?"

Escaping from her fears wouldn't make them go away. But dragging Cash into her problems wasn't fair to him.

Chapter Four

Cash finished his coffee in silence, patiently waiting for Stacey to open up. She had to confide in him of her own free will. She'd mentioned trouble and then shut down. Her emotions were all over the place, and he couldn't take advantage of her. Nor could he walk away.

She carried both cups to the kitchen and then set them on the counter, dropping to the couch next to him when she returned. Her expression was unreadable. He tried to see beneath the layer of bravado she was displaying.

Damn, he wanted to trust that she'd grown up and was no longer under her father's domineering thumb. Was her trouble stemming from family? Asserting her independence by supporting herself might have caused a major riff.

She rested her cheek on his shoulder. Having Stacey snuggled against him in a quiet apartment was a dream come true. He could've stayed in this setting forever. If only she'd talk to him. Why'd she think trouble had followed her?

"I'm sorry about Lance." Cash smoothed hair off her forehead, spreading the long, golden silk across her shoulder.

"Me too."

If she wasn't going to make this easy, he'd press her. "You ready to explain your earlier statement?"

Her body went rigid. Damned if the air in the room didn't cool significantly. In one motion, she scooted to the edge of the sleeper sofa. She'd turned her back to him, effectively closing him out.

"Look, sometimes I speak without thinking. Forget I said anything." She stood and planted her hands on her hips. "Maybe you should just go."

"Go?" A combo of confusion and alarm flashed through his system. "You have to trust somebody." He didn't want to leave, but he couldn't possibly stay. Not after she'd dismissed him.

"It's complicated."

Her cavalier gesture might've fooled somebody else. He didn't miss the anxiety behind her eyes and it ripped a hole in his gut. But she'd shut him out. He stood, pulled her into his arms, and kissed her soft lips. "I don't like leaving you alone. Call if you need me. Remember what I said. Anytime. Anywhere."

She didn't trust him enough to confide. That cut deep. Now he had to figure out how to fix that.

****

Today had been a struggle, but Stacey had managed to get through work without making too many mistakes. It had been a long eight hours.

Chiding herself for forgetting her sunglasses at home, she squinted in the bright sunlight. Shielding her eyes with her hand, she scanned her apartment's parking lot for anyone watching. She slipped her purse over her shoulder and headed up the stairs.

A shiver of excitement rushed over her just thinking about the deposit she'd made at the bank that day. Thursday was payday at the doctor's office, and between today's check and her tips from the weekend at the bar, her money worries had eased. The Rockin' Boot was a stop-gap measure, something to get her over the cash flow shortage. She'd heard the rumor Doc was considering hiring an office manager. If she worked hard and proved herself, she'd be the logical choice for the position.

She hadn't heard from Cash since sending him away Sunday. Her abrupt brush-off had upset him, but confiding in him wasn't a matter of trust. If Ray had killed Lance for hanging around her, being seen with her could cost Cash his life. She couldn't be sure it had been Ray but how could she take a chance? Her heart twisted. This situation had probably ended any chances of rebuilding a relationship with Cash.

She changed into shorts and a T-shirt then pulled the rubber band from her hair and dug her fingers into her scalp. Getting that weight off the back of her head was enough to make her lightheaded. She opened the vanity drawer and reached for her hairbrush.

"What?" she said, curious as hell that her comb, curling iron, and other products were there, but she couldn't locate her brush.

She checked the dresser, the nightstand, and every other available spot. Had she absentmindedly stuffed it in her purse? Stacey dumped the contents on her bed and sifted through the contents. She found a tube of lipstick she'd thought she'd lost, but no hairbrush.

She gave up the search and plopped down on the couch with a good book. Unable to concentrate, she dragged her hand through her tangled hair again. What had she been thinking involving Cash in her problems?

Lance's death had weakened her resolve. Her fear had tumbled away when Cash arrived and gathered her in his arms. Buried feelings had bubbled to the surface. Hell, who was she kidding? She had never really stopped thinking about him. Or wondering where he was, who he was with, and more importantly, if he was safe?

She'd hoped the rumor mill would answer those questions while she was at home. No way had she expected him to have moved back too.

He'd offered an olive branch, standing there all gorgeous in those blue jeans. Yet she'd steeled her heart and sent him home. If staying away from her kept him alive, then she'd made the right decision.

Her cell buzzed, bringing her focus to the present. She closed her book, realizing she couldn't remember a word she'd read. She checked caller ID and warmth spread over her. Cash.

"Hey." Surprised and relieved he'd called, she breathed a little easier.

"Sug," he said in that special tone that weakened her knees. "How about joining me for supper?" She heard no hint of anger at her earlier quick brush-off.

Her heart jumped to the back of her throat. Her emotions tugged her in one direction while logic pulled her in the other. She wanted to accept but feared for his safety.

"I promise not to pressure you for information."

If they stayed out of sight, would that be enough to keep him safe? Could she convince him to remain in the background until the killer was behind bars? The answer to that question was a resounding no.

"How about I come get you? We'll eat here, and you can check on the orphaned colt."

"I'd like that." Blood pulsed through her veins. Going to him was a better idea. "But I'll come to you. What can I bring?"

"Your appetite. Ginger is quite a cook. Supper's at six-thirty."

Stacey disconnected and then scrambled off the couch. She raced through the shower, applied fresh makeup, and hunted for her hairbrush again. She fished out an old one and finished her hair.

"Well, hell." She stared at the empty bowl on the breakfast bar where she usually put her sunglasses. The setting sun would be right in her line of vision on the drive to the ranch. She scanned the small kitchen and living room surfaces.

She'd misplaced her brush and her sunglasses. Was she getting feeble-minded? Paying so much attention to other things that she put her belongings down and couldn't remember where.

With no time to search, she checked to be sure she had her car keys and hurried out the door. She had to be sure no one followed her, so she circled through town a few times to make sure she didn't have a tail.

****

Cash hadn't asked why Stacey had been late for supper. She'd been withdrawn all through the meal. She handled her first visit to the ranch okay but they'd spent most of the time outside. Had eating in the dining room brought back sad memories of her mother's death?

As a teenager, he'd promised himself that someday he'd own a spread like this one. When he bought the old McKinney place, the possibility of Stacey ever sitting across the dining room table from him hadn't entered his mind. Or had it? Had his subconscious driven him to buy this place in hopes someday they'd raise a family right here where she grew up?

"Supper was delicious, Ginger. I know why Cash brags on you so much."

"He brags? Maybe I should ask for a raise." Ginger's robust laugh filled the room. "You two go on. I'll fix a pot of coffee before I leave."

He caught Ginger by the hand and stopped her. "No coffee. Your family is probably ready for you to come home."

She nodded. "See you tomorrow."

He turned to Stacey. The smile on her face relaxed him a little. He offered his hand. Heat shot up his arm when she rested her soft palm against his.

He needed to know what trouble drove her from the big city back to the country. Had fate brought her home to him? Could they recapture what they'd had so many years ago? He tamped down the twinge of hurt and irritation. Stacey had problems. Why was she being secretive? Didn't she know he'd want to help? She had no reason to distrust him.

Together they stepped off the porch and headed to the barn. The wind caught her long hair and blonde waves unfurled around her shoulders. Her lips curved upward into a smile and filled him with more light than the sun provided.

"I'm glad you came." He tugged, and she moved closer to him. He wrapped his arm around her shoulder, tightening his hold, molding her body against his. Could she feel how right this was?

"Sorry I was late."

"No problem." He breathed in her clean floral scent. He couldn't identify the flower; it wasn't roses or anything so ordinary.

"Ginger is a great cook."

"She's more like family. She'd befriended Mama long before I got out of the service. Sort of took it upon herself to fill in after Mama passed."

"I'm glad you have her." Stacey crossed the yard into the barn and went straight to the colt's stall. "He's going to have a beautiful red coat." She leaned over the gate and extended her hand for the young horse to sniff. "Is he eating enough?"

"I don't think so. The vet put him on additional vitamins."

"Where are your ranch hands?"

"Both of them have families. Everybody goes home at the end of the day. Ginger stayed because I had company coming."

Stacey wandered over to a bench that ran along the far wall. She sat, pulling her legs under her. Tall and slender, she had a childlike look about her. *A frightened child.* She took a deep breath and blew it out. Cash struggled to keep quiet. If she wanted to confide in him, it had to be her decision. She stared at her fingers, picking at an imaginary hangnail.

"I was the loan officer's assistant at a bank. This man, a regular customer, walked past my desk on the way in and out. Pleasant, he always spoke. One day, I'd gone next door for lunch. The place was crowded, so when he showed up at my table and asked if he could join me, I said sure. A few days later, he was there again."

She placed her hand on her stomach as if in pain, rolling Cash's insides into a ball.

"Go on." He wanted to hold her. Instead, he leaned against the wall, giving her space.

"Before the meal was over, he'd chastised me for being too friendly with the waiter. I got uncomfortable when he asked why I took so long in the restroom. So I excused myself and hurried back to work. The next day I looked up and he was at my desk with flowers. I refused them and explained I wasn't in the market for a relationship."

"He got angry." Cash's military training rushed to his hands. He flexed his fingers, forcing them to unclench.

"Not outwardly. He smiled, tossed the flowers in the trash, and left."

"But he didn't give up."

"Not even. Suddenly, he was everywhere. Parked outside my apartment. Leaning against the streetlight outside the bank. Then I started getting phone calls, which escalated to face-to-face confrontations. He said I'd intentionally led him on. I finally called the cops."

"Nothing they could do, right?"

"Not until I woke up one night with a knife pressed against my throat; I thought for sure he'd rape me. Instead, he lectured me. According to Ray, we were in love. Made for each other, and if he couldn't have me, no one would."

"Did the cops arrest him?" Cash relaxed his jaw when his teeth started hurting. Fear emanated from her. It washed over him feeding his need to protect her.

"Questioned and released. It was my word against his. I convinced a judge to issue a restraining order. Everybody knows how well those things work."

"That's why you came home?" That she'd been emotionally tormented by this maniac sent Cash's blood boiling.

"Yes. He knows nothing about my background. I thought Oak Hill would be safe. Not very smart of me to think he couldn't find me. I hoped he'd move on."

She swallowed. Cash got a bottle of water from the small refrigerator in the tack room and brought it to her.

"No one except Dad was supposed to know where I am. I swore him to secrecy by fabricating a story about needing to get back to my roots. He's pissed, but he'll honor my request."

The irony of them both returning to Oak Hill to find peace wasn't lost on Cash. "Your dad would be pissed if he knew I'd moved home too."

Her eyebrows dipped. "I can't imagine he'd care where you were."

Cash bit back a nasty retort about her domineering father, deciding to get back to the issue at hand. "You think this Ray found you."

"I think he may be here and has been following me." She ran her fingers through her hair, pulling a lock over her shoulder to inspect.

"Have you seen him?" Fire exploded in Cash's belly. He battled back the urge to pull her inside the safety of his arms.

"No...Maybe...I don't know." Frustration and confusion filled her tone. "At first, I figured I was jumping at shadows. Saturday night someone almost ran me off the road. I convinced myself it was a drunk driver. Thinking back, I'm not so sure."

"I want you to stay here until they figure out what's happening." The need to touch her was too much, so he pulled her hands into his. They were cool, soft, and small inside his big mitts.

"And put you, your ranch hands, and Ginger in danger? I can't do that."

"No one's going to hurt us." His heart jackhammered against his chest. Her behavior Sunday made sense now. She wanted to protect him. "What did Detective Kelly say about your suspicions?"

Her gaze dropped to the barn floor.

"You did tell them?"

"About Ray? No." She lifted her shoulders. "At the time, I didn't think the two were connected."

"Do you want me to talk with him?"

"No." She fired the answer back. "I can speak for myself."

"I wish you'd consider my offer to stay here."

Tears rimmed her eyes. She walked back to the colt's stall. Cash followed, letting her think about his offer.

"What if it was Ray, and he saw us together?"

"Let him come after me. He'll find me harder to kill than an inexperienced kid like Lance." Cash gripped her shoulders, turning her to face him. Fear emanated from her, slicing into him. The need to protect filled him "What's Ray's last name?"

"Simmons. Why?" Her eyes flashed wide. "Don't mess with him."

Cash stepped back, feigning shock. "Whoa. You don't think I can take care of myself? Talk about a blow to the ego.

Don't worry about me, I can handle myself." All the time he admonished her, he secretly hoped he'd get the chance to test his skills.

She moved closer and buried her face in his chest. His heart folded. He had to locate Ray. No way was the son of a bitch harming a hair on her head.

"If something happened to you..."

"I'll be fine." Cash lifted her chin with his fingers and thumbed away the tears from her beautiful face. "You're not responsible for this bastard's actions. You're not in this alone, and I won't let you down."

At that moment, with his statement, a realization hit Cash. He breathed in her scent, soaked up the warmth of her body, and released his anger. The past, with its real or imagined hurts, vanished from his mind.

Stacey wasn't responsible for her father's actions or how he'd treated the poor white trash boy who'd fallen in love with his daughter. No more than she should carry the guilt of Lance's death. Someday, he'd talk with her about the past. Right now, her life was in danger, and he'd watch over and protect her at all costs.

"I'd better get home. Brady has a popular band lined up for tomorrow night. I need to be at work early. Jonathan and I are double stocking our area."

"I can't convince you to stay?"

"I'll be extra careful." She smiled up at him. "Besides, it might not be smart for me to stay here so close to you."

He leaned down and touched his lips to hers. "Nice try at changing the subject. You leave me no choice but to follow you home."

"I can't ask you to do that."

"You didn't. Until I'm sure you're safe, I'll be there every night when you get off."

"Brady or Jonathan usually walks out with me and the other girls."

"Jonathan might be a nice guy, but no way is he capable of physically defending you."

"Just because he's not bulked up like you doesn't mean he—"

"I'm not saying he wouldn't try to protect you. Can we at least agree he's not your run of the mill hard-ass?"

"And you are?" Her eyes twinkled with the tease.

"When necessary? You damned right. So you think I've bulked up? Is that a good thing?"

"In your case? Definitely."

Cash slid his arm around her tiny waist and walked her out under the stars. The warm wind tossed her hair over her face, and he brushed it back. "I like the lighter shade. Why'd you change it?"

"Blondes are easier to find in the dark."

Chapter Five

Stacey made a second round through her apartment. Damn that she'd lost her sunglasses. Six-thirty at night and the sun was still a problem driving west. She didn't have time to pick up a new pair and still be on time for work at the bar. Giving up on her search, she headed down the stairs. The building manager, Sara Winston, was struggling to drag two large plastic bags toward the trash dumpster.

"Let me help with those." Stacey took one of them from the older woman and carried it down the steps.

"Thank you. They're heavier than I originally thought."

"No problem." Stacey lifted the lid on the dumpster and dropped one bag inside. The sun glinted off a piece of tinted glass and caught her attention. She reached in and pulled out a shard attached to a frame and then another. A shudder raced through her, leaving chill bumps on her arms and a knot in her stomach. Her broken sunglasses lay shattered in the garbage bin. "What the hell?"

Her heart sank to her feet. Only one way they wound up in the trash. Somebody had taken them from her counter and destroyed them.

Ray was in Oak Hill. The bastard had been inside her apartment.

"What is it?" Ms. Winston peeked around Stacey to get a look.

"These are mine, and I didn't break them or toss them." She shivered standing under the hot sun. Stacey whirled and scanned the parking lot. Her lungs seized. "Have you noticed a stranger hanging around?"

"No." Her landlady backed away as if she wanted to distance herself, but Stacey wasn't finished. Raw nerves sizzled with a combination of fear and fury.

"I believe somebody's been in my apartment."

"I didn't let anyone in." Ms. Winston's eyebrow rose.

"No," Stacey said. "I didn't think so. Somehow, they got in." How had Ray found her?

Cash was right. She had to share her fears with Sergeant Kelly. She dug out his business card, called, and succinctly gave him her history with Ray. She shared the Houston Detective's name and number in case Kelly wanted to follow up on her story. Relieved to have him in the loop, she explained finding her sunglasses. Ms. Winston stood close by. No doubt, she didn't want trouble at the apartment complex.

"Hang on." Stacey turned to her landlady.

"I have to get to work. Will you let the police in my place? Sergeant Kelly wants to take a look inside."

"With the proper identification, of course. You go ahead." Her gaze shifted giving Stacey the impression that she was frightened too.

"Tell her not to confront any strangers," Kelly said, apparently having overheard. "It could be dangerous."

****

Brady had been right, he'd predicted this band would draw a huge crowd and pack the bar. A steady stream of thirsty customers kept Stacey jumping. She'd done her best to forget about Ray, but she couldn't help scanning the crowd occasionally.

She emptied the tip jar so she and Jonathan could count the money. "Stocking the extra beer paid off."

"Looks like it to me," Brady said.

She jumped and slapped her hand over her heart. "Brady, you scared me." She'd lost count, so she pushed the money into a pile.

"Go ahead," he said, leaning against the counter. "I'll wait."

Stacey recounted the stack of money. She gave Jonathan his share and watched him head out, wishing her tired butt was right behind him. Brady didn't usually hang around and chat. He'd stop by and check in, occasionally asking when her dad was coming for a visit. Tonight he'd almost hovered. Lance's murder had upset him too.

"What's up?" she asked, making one final swipe before joining him on the other side of the bar counter.

"We haven't had a chance to talk. You doing okay?" His frown lines were deeper, more like worry grooves.

She opened her mouth and then closed it. Even if Ray had followed her, he was too smart to come inside the bar and cause trouble.

"No answer means you're not okay." Brady leaned closer. "Maybe you should call your dad. He'd be here in a flash."

"I'm tired. Otherwise, I'm fine. And I can't call my father every time something upsets me." She hoped she'd gotten her point across. She didn't need Brady tracking down her dad and dragging him into this mess.

"She doesn't need Russell," Cash said from behind her, "I'm here and nothing will happen to her on my watch." He draped an arm over her shoulder. "You ready?"

"I am if the boss says so." She stood, leaned into Cash, and waited for Brady to respond.

A smile spread across his face. "Looks like you've got all the help you need right here." He shook Cash's hand. "Glad to see you two together. I was hoping Russell hadn't caused a permanent rip." He motioned toward the exit. "You two go on."

"What kind of crack was that?" Baffled by Brady's reference to her father, she started after him. Cash's hand on her arm stopped her.

"Come on, Sug. Let's get you out of here." Cash dropped a soft kiss on her forehead. "You have to be exhausted."

"I'm whipped, but he shouldn't say stuff like that about my father and just walk away."

"We'll worry about that later."

Knowing Cash had made a trip to town because of her, warmed her to her toes. She put her night's tips in her purse, slid her arm around his waist, and snuggled close on the way to her car.

"Thank you for watching over me." She went up on her tiptoes to kiss him goodnight.

He buzzed her lips. "I'm following you home. I'll collect a decent kiss once you're inside your apartment." He opened her car door and stepped back. The smile that turned her insides to liquid slid across his face.

"Are you coming in?"

"You're safe for tonight. I like my women awake."

Under the full moon, she waited until he got behind the wheel of his pickup. Was she falling in love with him all over again? Had she ever stopped? It didn't matter. He couldn't be trusted. Who knew when he'd up and disappear again?

****

Police cars surrounded Stacey's apartment so thick that Cash had to park a block away. Her curiosity ran wild on the walk to the entry gate. Oak Hill didn't have a large police department. Based on the number of cruisers surrounding the building, they were all here.

Cash shook hands with the cop who'd been assigned to keep anyone from entering the premises. "We need to get into two-twelve."

"Not gonna happen for a while."

"I live here," she said quickly. She lifted to her tip toes trying to see what was happening.

"I heard you'd come home." The cop stepped in front of her, blocking her line of vision.

Stacey looked closer at the man. "Bubba Henry? Is that you?" His head moved forward slightly, indicating she was right.

"I'm surprised to see you back in our hick town," he said with a hint of humor. "Wait here." He moved to the other side of his cruiser and spoke into the microphone clipped to his shirt.

What the heck? First Brady and now Bubba? Was it her imagination or were the men in town talking gibberish? Why wouldn't she come home?

"Think maybe my landlady spotted Ray hanging around and called the cops?" She inched closer to the walk-through gate to her stairs.

An ambulance emerged moving slowly from the complex parking lot. No lights. No siren.

"Could be. This many cops wouldn't show up for a routine break-in," Cash said.

Bubba motioned them to join him. "Wait here. Sergeant Kelly wants to talk with you."

"Can't you tell us what happened?"

"No." Bubba shook his head. "Sarge would peel the flesh off my bones. He'll tell you when he's ready."

Cash led her back to the sidewalk. "I wish you'd rethink staying at the ranch."

The seriousness in his gaze touched her. "If you're sure, I'll take you up on your offer. Too many unexplainable things have happened. I believe Ray's been inside my apartment." She told him about her brush and sunglasses. Judging by the nerve in his jaw, he thought she was right.

"You should have told me. It's settled. If he got in once, he can do it again." The nerves in Cash's jaw twitched.

"I'm sorry to have dragged you into my mess."

"Don't you know? I belong in whatever *mess* you're in." Cash tilted his head sideways, leaned down, and covered her lips with his.

The fire started slowly, rolling through her, filling her with joy. In the middle of the chaos, she'd found her anchor. The universe settled into its proper rotation. At least for a moment, she belonged here.

"I do know," she whispered. "Maybe fate brought me home because you're here."

"We'll get your clothes and move you tonight."

"If Ray is in town, the less you're seen with me the better off you'll be."

Sergeant Kelly called her name. He walked past the gathering crowd toward her and Cash. His expression grew grimmer each time his foot hit the pavement. Stacey had the impression from their prior meeting that he was all business when on the job.

"Did you speak with Ms. Winston after you called me today?" He'd wasted no time on pleasantries.

"No. I left for work. Did she let you in my apartment?"

"Yes. I didn't see anything unusual, I asked her a couple of questions and then left."

"But something strange has happened. What is it?"

"She's dead."

"No," Stacey gasped and stumbled back a step. Shock quickly morphed into anger. "What happened?"

"A tenant found her at the bottom of the stairs. Her neck was broken."

"No way," Stacey argued.

"The medical examiner will make the final determination, but I'm inclined to agree with you. I need a little more information on your stalker." The sergeant waved toward the back seat of a cruiser. "Step into my office and let's talk."

****

Cash listened to Bubba but kept a watchful eye on Stacey. Kelly was a newcomer in Oak Hill. Whether he was good at his job or not had yet to be proven. Cash wasn't in the mood to cut him any slack. Not where Stacey was concerned.

She'd leaned back in the cruiser, making Cash shift positions to keep her in his line of sight. He couldn't hear her words, but her hands moved rapidly while she talked. The longer she stayed with Kelly, the tighter the nerves between Cash's shoulder blades knotted. After what felt like hours, Stacey emerged. She stretched her arms over her head and then dragged her hand through her hair. Kelly followed her back to where Cash and Bubba stood talking.

"I understand you've offered Ms. McKinney a place to stay. I think that's a good idea." Kelly handed his card to Cash. "I'd like your phone number. Just in case I can't reach Ms. McKinney."

Cash jotted down his home and cell information then passed the card back. "When can we get inside her apartment?"

"I'll walk you up." Kelly glanced at Stacey. "I'd like to take a look around. Be good for you to do the same; see if anything else is missing."

"Lead the way," she said.

She grasped Cash's hand and tugged as if to say, come with us. He squeezed back. No way was she getting out of his sight.

Kelly tried the door and found it locked. Stepping back, he waved Stacey forward. "Appears to be secure. Go ahead and open it."

Cash caught the look she shot in his direction. Words weren't necessary. Stacey was frightened out of her wits. Cash took her keys, unlocked the door, and entered first.

"Son of a bitch. Kelly, take a look at this." Cash stood between her and the doorway. Damn it.

"What did you see?" She pushed past far enough to get an eyeful. "My God."

"Stay here." Kelly drew his pistol and stepped into the destruction.

Cash bit back the urge to follow. Protecting Stacey was more important. A few minutes later, Kelly waved them inside.

Unsure how she'd react, Cash had held Stacey tightly. He didn't figure her for the fainting kind, but he'd stay on the safe side. Her living room looked like a hand grenade had exploded. The couch was in shreds and the one easy chair lay on its side a long slash ran across the headrest. Magazines and broken glass were scattered across the floor.

She broke away and ran into her bedroom. "My clothes."

Stacey dropped to the floor. She gathered the tossed about and torn pieces of clothing tightly against her chest. Tears trickled down her cheeks.

His heart crunched. She'd always carried her head high, but everyone had their breaking point. He feared she'd reached hers.

Cash squatted next to her. "You probably shouldn't pick things up. Kelly will need everything left as is."

"He's right," Kelly said. "Maybe your guy did locate you. I'm assuming this place was intact when you left." He stuck his head in the bathroom, stepped right back out, and then motioned for her to join him.

If for no other reason than to give himself something to do, Cash kept his arm around her waist. He'd felt this kind of anger before, had wanted to kill somebody with his bare hands, but that had been war. Well, the son of a bitch who'd done this damage had declared his brand of warfare. Cash would answer that call too.

Scrawled across the mirror with lipstick were the words, "Now you're dead."

"It's Ray. He's crazier than I thought." Stacey paled, and Cash pulled her closer.

"I need you two to wait outside," Kelly announced. "If you want to hang around until we sort this out, fine. Or I can call you when you can come back."

"I need clothes." Stacey balked.

"We'll get you some new things tomorrow." Cash steered her toward the hall. "For now, let's go to the ranch. You're dead on your feet."

"Last chance to withdraw your offer." Her gaze locked on his. The fear in her eyes cut a hole in his chest. "Be sure."

"I am." His heart double-clutched at the frustration and underlying terror in her voice. "For what it's worth, I intend to keep you safe."

She glanced over her shoulder at the carnage. "That means more to me than you can imagine." She lowered her gaze to her feet. "If Ms. Winston and Lance were killed because of me, you could be in real danger. I feel guilty asking you to risk your life."

"You're not. I volunteered." Cash gathered her in his arms and crushed her to his chest. Her sad eyes and downturned lips had ripped him apart. Leaning down, he slid his thumb under one of her eyes, catching a single tear that had escaped. "It's late. Let's go home."

Chapter Six

The phrase "Let's go home," replayed in Stacey's head, wrapping around her like one of her mother's homemade quilts. She'd never heard sweeter words. She tucked them away in her heart for safekeeping.

She prayed they'd find Ray before he did any more harm. No one else could die because of her. The thought of putting Cash and his employees in danger turned her stomach into a churning caldron.

"Hey." Cash's fingers on her cheek sent a warm shudder through her system. "Where'd you go?"

"If something happens to you because of me..." She swallowed back the rest of the sentence. He'd just brush off her concerns and worry more about her safety than his own.

"Nothing's going to happen." His tone was self-assured and confident.

"I hope you're right. Locating Ray would clear up a few questions. I don't think Dad would break his promise and tell anyone I'd moved home, but I have to call and ask."

Cash jerked his hand away as if touching her shocked him.

"There's no need to involve him." Cash parked next to the house, turning to face her. "Unless you want your dad to come to Oak Hill."

"You're probably right." The dark tone of Cash's voice troubled her. What was he not saying? Would he tell her if she asked? No way. He couldn't be forced to open up. Waiting until he was ready was going to be difficult.

The house was dark except for one exterior light. Memories of sitting out on the porch counting fireflies rushed her. She was thrilled he'd bought this place and made it his own.

He unlocked the door and led her down the hall, stopping outside her old bedroom.

"You okay staying in here?"

"Of course." She opened the door and flipped on the light unsure what she'd see. The room was a pleasant surprise.

Decorated in various shades of pastel green and white oak furniture, a wicker chair occupied the space her old lounger used to fill. The space resembled a picture from a Better Homes and Garden spread. "It's lovely."

"I can't take credit for it. Ginger got tired of it setting empty and this is the result. She missed her calling."

"I think so, but aren't you lucky?"

"Wait." His arm slipped around her shoulder. "I should have my ass kicked for not realizing this room would have too many memories. Come to one of the other guest rooms."

"No. This is fine." A strange sadness settled on her heart. Did he consider her just another guest? "You don't want me to sleep with you?"

"More than you can imagine." His gray eyes darkened like storm clouds. "But when or if you come to my bed, I want you to plan on staying. One hundred percent positive that's where you need to be. We're not kids any longer, I want more."

She stood mesmerized by the man in front of her. He was right. She hadn't had a rational thought since hearing Ms. Winston was dead. Bone tired and scared out of her wits wasn't conducive to making good decisions.

"Thank you."

He pulled her against his rock hard chest and held her for a long second. He'd done that a lot over the past few hours, offering support and protection. She couldn't find words to tell him how much that simple action meant to her.

"I'll probably be in the barn when you get up." His finger hooked under her chin, lifting until her gaze met his. "You'll come down?"

"Sure." She could've stayed inside his strong arms forever, but after a soft brush of his lips, he was gone and she was alone with her thoughts.

She undressed for bed, fighting back the depression of probably being responsible for two people lying in the morgue. The reality of the possibility pressed hard on her heart.

She slipped between the sheets, thinking the soft colors of the room were soothing. She was safe here with Cash. Tall, proud, and successful Cash. A very different person than the boy she'd known. The horse ranch made her think he'd come home to stay, but had he?

Outside, Crickets sang, lulling her to sleep. She drifted off, wondering if this was firefly season.

****

The aroma of cinnamon had pulled her out of a troubled sleep earlier than she normally rose on the weekend. It afforded her not only the chance to eat the best sweet roll she'd ever had, but she'd spent time with Cash's housekeeper, Ginger. Short and round with a twinkle in her eyes, she'd chatted and laughed like she and Stacey were old friends.

She made the short walk to the barn remembering mornings when it would've been her dad she was hunting. She entered the building and forgot about the past. Cash was backing out of a stall pulling a wheelbarrow. Her mind whirled at the sight before her. His shirt, damp with sweat, clung to him, outlining his muscular stomach and shoulders.

"Morning, Sug."

His words slid down her spine, sending chill bumps across her skin. He removed his western hat and leather gloves and then wiped the sweat from his brow. She concentrated her energy on delivering the iced tea she'd brought him.

"For me? Careful you'll spoil me." He took the glass and then drank the contents without coming up for air.

"I can't take credit. Ginger sent it."

"Her method of delivery has improved." He settled his hat back in place. "Did you sleep okay?"

"Like a rock. Something about this place always made me feel safe." She rose on tiptoes for a kiss. "Might've been because you were just down the hall."

"Hmm." He smiled down at her from under the brim of his hat. "Knowing you were that close had the opposite effect on me." He eased into her space, lowering his face close to hers. "I smell cinnamon."

"Ginger saved me a roll. I love her by the way." "Good. 'Cause she's got a heart as big as Texas."

"I could tell." Stacey glanced around the barn. "This place must take a lot of work. Where are your ranch hands?"

"Ramon's gone to town to pick up a load of feed, and Henry's around here somewhere." An impish grin slid across Cash's face. "We're not alone, but I could arrange it."

Heat churned low in her belly every time he dropped his voice to that sexy whisper. "I do have a few hours before I have to be at work. Don't tempt me."

"But I like tempting you." He moved back to the wheelbarrow, slipped on his gloves, and lifted it without effort. "Let me put this away then I'm finished for a while. I had a text from Kelly this morning. He'll meet us at your apartment and let you pass the crime scene tape to gather a few things. Anything else you need, we'll go shopping and buy."

"I'll try to piece together enough to get by, but I need my boots. Do you think Kelly will tell us if he's learned anything about Ray?"

"Probably not. But we're going to ask. Let me dump this manure and get back to the house. I'll call Ash Hunter."

"Who is he?"

"An old Army buddy. He's a detective with the Houston police department. I'll ask him to covertly dig into Ray's past and whereabouts."

"That would be wonderful." She leaned against a stall gate and watched Cash finish his work.

A myriad of emotions swirled through her with every ripple of his muscles. He triggered surges of hormones, flirted shamelessly, and bent over backward to watch over her. Still, she couldn't read behind that storm cloud in his eyes. He'd said he'd want more if they made love. How much more? Was he hinting at a commitment? Could she trust him with her heart? Or should she protect herself?

"Hello?" Cash towered over her. An I-caught-you-daydreaming smile lifted the corners of his mouth.

Wow. She was losing it. He'd finished and was ready to walk her back to the house. Must be fear bouncing her emotions and decisions back and forth.

"Sorry, my mind wandered." She fought back the rush of blood to her cheeks.

"You're beautiful when you daydream. I hope your thoughts had wandered to me." He coiled his fingers around hers. "Come on, I need to grab a quick shower."

Was it the sun or Cash that warmed her heart on the walk to the house? Stacey was pretty sure she knew the answer to that question.

Cash left her at the guest bedroom door and headed for the bathroom. She curled up in the wicker chair next to the bed to wait. She considered joining him but remembered her dad didn't have her new phone number. She could at least give that to him. She grabbed her throwaway cell and dialed his number. Wait until he heard where she was staying. Talk about irony.

"Hey, Dad."

"Stacey? Where the hell are you?" he snapped in his typical angry tone.

"In Oak Hill, right where I told you I'd be."

Then why haven't you returned my calls?" He'd gotten angry when she announced her decision to move home. She was hoping his new wife had changed his mood.

"I am sorry. I changed phones and forgot to tell you. It's been hectic here." She hoped *hectic* would suffice. She rattled off the new number. "So, how are you? How's Marie? I don't have long to talk."

"She's fine. When are you moving back to Houston?"

Stacey ignored his question hoping not to rehash an old argument. "Guess who bought our old home place and turned it into a horse ranch?"

"I'm not interested in playing games. Who are we talking about?"

"You remember Cash Butler?"

"Of course, I know that white trash. The bastard kid's mama didn't have two dimes to rub together. How'd he pull off a deal like that?"

"What a horrible thing to say." His tone shocked her. He'd always been opinionated and a bit of a snob, but this was an unexpected ugly side of him. "Cash has worked hard to fix up the place." She glanced around at the decor of the room. "In fact, I'm here right now."

The line went silent. She had enough problems without him being unreasonable. "Hello?"

"What has he told you?"

"About what?"

"Never mind. Just stay away from him."

"Why would I? And why are you acting this way?"

"Butler's why you moved back to Oak Hill, isn't he? I'll not have that bastard worming his way into this family. You get your ass back to Houston."

"Stop it. I'm not a kid that you can order around, and I'm not coming back," Stacey snapped out of frustration. Her father had always tried to pick her friends, but his attitude toward Cash was beyond her understanding.

He grunted something Stacey could hardly make her mind believe what she'd heard. She picked out the words 'should've sent him to jail.'

"Wait a minute." Realization swept across like wildfire. "Talk to me, Dad. What did you do?" Everything fell into place. Cash's negative reaction when the subject of her father came up. Brady's and Bubba's comments. They knew something she didn't. "I mean it. Tell me."

"I did what any good father would've done. I made damn sure he stayed away from you. I'll not apologize for saving you from a life of poverty."

"He's why we moved? Dad, how could you?" Her question was met with silence. "I'm sorry. I can't talk to you right now."

She ended the call and stared out the window not knowing whether to cry or rage against the injustice. Her heart weighed heavy in her chest. All this time wasted. All this time, she'd blamed Cash for running out on her. She dropped her head to her hands and cried tears for the lost years.

The faint scent of soap and woodsy cologne pulled her attention to the open doorway. His long legs carried him across to her. Concern furrowed his eyebrows.

"What's wrong?"

"I know what my father did to you. To us." The pain of betrayal swamped her, flooding her cheeks. "He drove you away. Didn't he?"

He knelt in front of her and thumbed away her tears. "It's history. Forgotten. You're here with me now, and that's all that matters." His facial expression revealed nothing.

"It's not forgotten. How could you not blame me? I certainly blamed you."

"Nonsense."

The young Cash had been talkative and open. The grownup version seemed unwilling to talk about the past. Stacey had to understand what happened so long ago.

"I thought you'd abandoned me. Disappeared, preferring the military to me. At least that's what I was told over and over."

Cash stared out the window for a long time. Had she pushed too hard?

"Will you tell me what happened?"

He faced her. Thunderclouds stirred behind his gray eyes.

"He treated my mother like scum. Brought the sheriff out to the house with him and scared the shit out of her. Maybe she wasn't rich or educated or wise to the ways of the world, but she'd worked hard to take care of me. He intended to trump up a charge against me if I didn't 'disappear.' She begged me to enlist. I was just young and stupid enough to do it."

"I'm sorry. Sorry for the pain he caused. Sorry for the time we lost."

He cupped her cheek with his hand and covered her lips with his. A kiss of forgiveness? Understanding? Or avoidance? He increased the pressure, sliding his tongue inside her mouth.

Her heart did a backflip. She marveled at her body's instant reaction to him. Her breasts ached to be touched. Her hands itched to run over his chest muscles. His black hair was still damp. The blue button-down collared western shirt and blue jeans he wore outlined every muscle.

She pulled back, studying his face for signs that he could move forward, and prayed she wasn't giving her heart away just to get it stomped on.

"You're looking at me like I'm the blue plate special again. You're gonna give me a complex."

"I am not." She smiled when he chuckled. A piece of her anger melted.

A second kiss took her breath away. All she could think of was how much fun it would be to lick him from head to toe. To slowly run her tongue over every inch of his body. How would he react to that?

"I'd love every minute."

"Every minute of what?" Heat raced up her chest and scorched her cheeks. "I said that licking part out loud, didn't I?"

"Yeah. Sounds like a good plan to me."

He stood, pulling her up with him. Nuzzling the side of her neck, he trailed tiny kisses up to her forehead and came down her nose until he found her lips. This kiss wasn't gentle. This kiss demanded surrender. Her legs buckled, and she crumbled into his arms.

"How the hell do you do that?" she asked when they finally came up for air. "You effectively changed the subject. We need to talk."

"I prefer action."

He'd won this round. But the hurt hadn't healed and she had to figure a way to help him. With a sigh, she went back for another sample of his lips. She clung to him, needing his body pressed against hers. Feeling him hard against her was intoxicating, powerful, and erotic as hell.

Grasping at what sanity she had left, she tried to rein in her desire. "Thank you for believing me."

His fingertips traced the line running down her jaw to her chin. "You've haunted my waking thoughts and given me dreams that made me want to sleep forever. I'm glad you know." He covered her mouth with his and swept his tongue inside.

Stacey pulled away, pleased by the look of disappointment in his gaze. She closed the door and turned to face him, delighted by his groan.

His hands slid under her shirt, cupping her breasts, snapping her hormones to attention. He lifted her blouse, tossed it in the chair, and then one-handed the hook on her bra.

"Oh, Sug." He pushed the straps from her shoulders, freeing her breasts. "You are not a dream."

He leaned down, took her nipple in his mouth, and sucked greedily. A deep rumble eased from his throat, and electricity shot straight from her breast to her very core.

"Your breasts are addicting. I'll never tire of touching you, of tasting you."

His words melted her heart. It expanded in her chest and pounded against her ribs so hard she wondered if he could hear it.

"Then don't stop," she whispered.

He kissed her jawline drawing tiny designs with the tip of his tongue on her neck. Pushing her backward, they moved one step at a time until she bumped into the bed.

He finished undressing her. His gaze followed his hands. His lips kissed bare skin. Desire changed to need, weakening Stacey's knees.

He pulled at his shirt, but she caught his hands, pushing them to his sides. "Wait. Let me."

She tugged at his jeans until he stopped her long enough for him to toe off his boots. Slowly, she studied his amazing body. He was perfect. His lean, muscular body looked as if an artist sculpted it from granite, and luckily, the same guy had carved his face.

She dragged him down beside her. Kissing his cheeks, she worked her way down his neck. Her lips roved and her tongue tasted with small flicks. The muscles and texture of his body were works of art.

"Enough," he growled, grabbing for his wallet and fumbling with the foil packet.

"Give that to me." She held back a laugh at his fascination and slid the condom on him.

He rolled her to her back and then lowered his hips between her thighs. He kissed his way downward to her breasts. His tongue left a trail of fire in its path. He reached her belly button, circled it, and drew patterns before he crept lower. The flame of need grew into a raging fire. Her skin started to tighten and burn.

"Cash." It was barely a whisper, but she was ready to plead for more.

His tongue brought about a quake inside her mind, body, and soul. Mercilessly he devoured her until she cried out in an explosion of joy.

"You're so beautiful," he whispered.

He entered her with a quick thrust. His penetration reached deep into her heat. Sensations ricocheted through her body. Needing more, she began to move under him.

She grabbed his shoulders and cried, "I'm coming. Come with me."

He moved faster, harder, driving her deeper and deeper toward the edge. Waves pulled her under, and she surrendered her heart to him. She gripped him tightly, matching his movements until he joined her in the sea of release.

She smiled when he rolled to the side, taking her with him. "You're beautiful too."

"Men aren't beautiful," he protested, but she recognized the gleam in his eyes.

He tunneled his fingers through her hair. His gaze drifted lazily across her face. A slight lifting of his lips made her curious.

"What are you thinking?"

"There's this look in your eyes when I'm inside you. I can't describe it."

"Is it weird?"

"Far from it. Your expression is the most erotic thing I've ever seen. It's like having me inside you is where I belong."

"Maybe it is." She leaned over him and kissed the tip of his nose.

"You may be right." He licked the tip of her nipple. "Do you have to go to work? I'm fine with staying right here all day."

"Yes. We have to stop by my apartment. I'll jump in the shower and then head to the bar."

"You're not going to go...what did you call it? Ah yes, 'Billy-Bad-Ass' on me if I offer to drive you to and from?"

She rolled away and reached for her clothes. His fingers trailed down her bare bottom, pulling a laugh from her. "Would it do any good?"

"No."

The sound of his zipper drew her attention. His hands were rough, calloused from working, yet gentle when they touched her. She'd always measured men against him, maybe not intentionally, but none had met the standard he'd set as a young man. She'd finally accepted the fact nobody ever would.

Chapter Seven

Cash made it to the hood of his pickup before he let the laugh escape. Stacey, on the other hand, appeared to be struck speechless ever since she'd remembered Ginger being in the house. Stacey's fear the sounds of sex had been overheard had left her at a loss for words.

"It's not funny," Stacey protested. Pink flooded her cheeks, rushing to her hairline.

"Sug, the kitchen's too far away from the bedroom for her to have heard you cry out my name."

"You're just saying that." Her tone resonated with hope. "Aren't you?"

"Yeah." He couldn't resist teasing her. "You do have a set of lungs on you."

The blow to his arm brought a laugh from them both. He laid his open hand on the passenger side door handle. She touched his face, stopping him. Big blue eyes sparkled in the sunlight. At that moment, the broken pieces of his life came together. With her, two sides made a whole.

"Ginger grocery shops on Saturday."

"Is that the truth?" She squeezed his fingers.

"I'll always be honest with you."

He opened the pickup door, and Stacey lifted a foot to the running board.

The sound he heard was distinct. Blood-curdling.

Deadly. There was no other like it.

The rattle was a warning. Time stopped.

Stacey froze.

Adrenaline slammed into Cash's system. The snake struck at the same time he looped an arm around her waist and jerked her behind him. He put a boot on the door and kicked it closed, locking it to keep anyone else from opening it.

He turned to face her, pulling her rigid body against his. Seconds later, she trembled from head to toe. He tipped her face up to find the color had drained from her skin, and her pupils were dilated.

"It's okay. Breathe. I've got you." Afraid she'd gone into shock, he scooped her into his arms and hurried to the porch. "Stacey. Talk to me."

"I'm going to be sick."

"Go ahead."

"Put me down."

No way was she getting very far from him. He put her feet on the ground and followed as she rushed to his shrubs where she lost the contents of her stomach. When her heaves subsided, he guided her inside.

He helped her to the couch, tucking a blanket around her to stop her shivers. He wanted to hold her, to kiss away the memory of the rattlesnake, but calls had to be made.

His chat with the 911 operator was brief. Because his ranch was outside the city limits he expected both the locals and a deputy sheriff to show up.

The next call went to Ash Hunter a detective friend in Houston. Cash wanted firsthand information on Ray Simmons right away. He'd explain the situation to Ash with confidence that the information would be forthcoming.

"Is this the same Stacey you used to talk about?" Ash never forgot anything, which sometimes wasn't a good thing. He could ferret out anyone's deepest secrets.

"Yeah." Cash smiled at the beauty resting on his couch. Her color had returned. Now instead of frightened, she looked pissed. "Hang on I'm putting you on speaker."

He made introductions and turned the call over to Ash who let Stacey do most of the talking. The longer she spoke the stronger she sounded, so Cash went to his house phone and called the barn, instructing his two ranch hands to come to the house. It was only right to give them a chance to opt out of working for a few days.

Stacey's laughter from the other room put a smile on his face. No telling what that dog Ash was saying. Cash decided he'd better get closer to the phone and rejoin the conversation.

"So, did Cash tell you I was a rescuer of damsels in distress?"

"He failed to mention that." She scooted over, making room for him to sit.

"What else did you tell her?" Cash asked, bracing for Ash's usual line of bull.

The room went silent for a heartbeat before Ash responded. "Only that you saved my life."

"And you returned the favor."

"I'll see what I can find out on Ray Simmons. In the meantime, watch your six."

The line went dead. Never one to talk about his heroics as a Ranger, Ash had reverted to business.

Cash stood after hearing voices outside. "I'm going to send Ginger and my men home for a few days. Just until we stop this lunatic."

"I'll talk to them." She folded the blanket and rose to her feet. "The least I can do is apologize."

"Not necessary." Sirens ended their discussion. "If you'll explain to Kelly what we found in the pickup, I'll take care of the boys."

"I'll meet him on the porch." She stopped at the door and cut him a glance from the corner of her eyes. "No way I'm getting near that pickup."

Her smile and wisecrack lightened the weight resting on Cash's shoulders. This was one tough woman. His respect for her grew daily.

****

Tempted to check for steam coming from her ears, Stacey shifted sideways and lifted her feet beside her on the porch swing. Sergeant Kelly had told her to stay out of the way. As if she were stupid enough to get within a city block of that snake.

Creepy crawly sensations skittered around under her skin. One of the sheriff's deputies was a snake wrangler, catching rattlesnakes for the big roundup in Sweetwater every year. He removed a long metal rod from his trunk and had everyone back away.

A person had to be insane to catch a viper so deadly and then put it in Cash's floorboard. A shiver raced through her. If she'd moved a second faster getting into the truck, she'd have been bitten and would be in the hospital fighting for her life.

A thought hit. Her stomach lurched.

What if she wasn't the target? Had the snake been placed on the driver's side of the pickup? It could've easily slithered across the mat.

Stacey's heart imploded. She couldn't put him at risk. Not again. For his sake, she had to stay away from him. Her mind raced in search of a workable plan.

Cash stepped onto the porch. Picking up her feet, he sat next to her, placing them on his lap. His dark eyes held a hint of anger, but he said nothing. The wind caught his woodsy scent, sending a gentle touch across her skin and calming her. Leaving him would be the hardest thing she'd ever done. His safety came first.

After this nightmare ended, would he welcome her back? The idea of losing him for the second time filled her soul with darkness. He might not be in her arms, but he'd be alive.

She dropped her feet to the floor. "There's nothing left for the cops to ask, so I'm going home."

"Come again? I must not have understood you."

The look of confusion on his face ripped at her heart. "Please don't argue. Ray knows I'm here."

"And he damn near killed you." Cash's harsh tone sent chills across her skin. "There's not much left of your apartment. You're not going back there alone. In fact, until this bastard is caught or I kill him, you're not going anywhere alone."

Kill him? Judging from the expression on Cash's face, he was capable of doing just that. All the more reason to relieve him from the burden of trying to protect her.

"Don't tell me what to do. If you'd try being logical, you'd know I'm right." Unable to face him with any more lies, she turned her back and went inside.

Cash caught up with her in the hall. Strong hands lightly gripped her shoulders, weakening her resolve. Was her leaving stupid? Probably. But he'd placed himself in mortal danger because of her.

"Sug," he whispered into her hair, almost melting her resolve. "Don't you know I'd lose my mind from worry if you left? Please, don't make me live out of my truck just to watch over you."

"I can't let you risk your life."

He sucked in a deep breath. "It's possible the rattlesnake was supposed to bite me. But it could've been placed there for you."

Tears streamed down her cheeks, tears for how helpless this situation made them. Tears for all those years they'd lost. She turned into his arms. The pressure in her heart to speak up was too much to bear. With her face buried against his chest, she whispered, "I love you."

There, she'd said it. She'd released an elephant in the room. Had she made a fool out of herself? She held her breath waiting for him to say something. Anything.

He hooked his finger under her chin and tugged until she looked up. His gaze locked onto hers. He tenderly brushed her cheeks dry. Panic that she'd said too much rushed her. The blood ran from her head. He'd said he wanted more. But how much more?

The corners of his mouth lifted, and his stormy eyes sparkled. Hope flared inside her chest.

"That's a good thing. 'Cause I never stopped loving you."

He cupped her cheek with his hand, lowered his head, and pressed his lips against hers. Tender and touching, his mouth made promises without words.

"Please don't leave. Stay and let's fight Ray together."

Her insides liquefied. Life wouldn't be cruel enough to separate them twice. Peace wrapped around her, stealing her voice. All she could do was nod.

"And don't be afraid of what we're feeling. If problems come up, we'll handle them."

She nodded again, knowing she should answer, to respond and say he was right. A huge lump had formed in her throat. He loved her too. Nothing, ab-so-lute-ly nothing, else mattered. Once they healed the damage her father had caused, and Cash got past his hate, she would see trust in his eyes too.

Cash slipped his arm around her waist, and together they went back outside. For the first time, she noticed how beautiful the day had turned out. Blue skies, the hot Texas sun, and a slight breeze, who could ask for more?

Then she spotted his pickup with the doors wide open. The snake wrangler who'd caught that rattler deserved a pat on the back. No way could she get in that truck again.

"You are trading in that pickup, aren't you?"

"First thing tomorrow."

****

The bar was having a busy night, but so far, Stacey had stayed in his line of sight. Cash leaned forward, keeping a watchful eye on her. He shifted, making sure the Sig Sauer under his shirt stayed hidden. He wasn't worried about breaking the law by bringing a weapon into the bar. Her safety came first.

Earlier today, Cash had questioned his hearing. Stacey saying I love you could only be compared to being struck by lightning. His years of discontent had vanished.

Other than to his mother, Cash had never uttered those words. Yet, they'd rolled off his tongue with no effort, leaving him in complete peace.

He'd tried to convince Stacey not to go to work. The argument had ended when she'd agreed to him being sequestered in the far corner. The spot he'd selected gave him optimum observation capabilities and a straight line to her workstation. He could be at her side in seconds.

The night progressed slowly. She made a mad dash to the ladies' room, which brought a smile to his face and took him back to the night he'd seen her for the first time in years. When she returned, she wiggled her fingers and held up an empty tray. That was her way of saying she and Jonathan had to restock. Cash hated her being out of sight, but he gritted his teeth and ten minutes of hell later, she returned carrying sliced lemons and limes while Jonathan wheeled in cases of beer.

When the overhead lights flashed last call, Cash breathed a sigh of relief. Stacey would start cleaning the minute the crowd cleared out. He stood, straightened his shirt, and headed for her station.

"Hello, gorgeous." He dropped a kiss on her forehead.

She smiled, but her nerves were strung tight. Faint circles under her eyes hinted she hadn't been sleeping well. How long could they keep this up?

"Back at ya." She hoisted an empty tray on top of another. "Be right back. I gotta take these to Jonathan."

Cash sensed someone had walked up behind him. Spinning on his heels, he almost cold-cocked Brady. "Don't sneak up on me," Cash growled.

"Sorry," Brady said, backing up a step. "I'm glad you're here. I have to talk to Stacey, and she's not going to like what I say."

"What's that?"

"Everybody in town has heard about her apartment being trashed. The buzz around the pool tables this afternoon was the rattler in your truck." Brady scrubbed a hand across his chin. "I don't need that kind of trouble."

Cash regretted not accidentally decking the man when he'd had the chance. "You're firing her?"

"What am I supposed to do? Hire armed guards in case the next surprise is a sack full of copperheads released in here?"

"It was a rattler and you're being ridiculous. The only person who should be scared is Stacey. Hell, she's got more balls than you."

"It's not unreasonable to protect my customers." Brady backed up and sat on a stool. "Where'd she go?"

Cash whirled the direction she'd gone. His heart leaped to the back of his throat. Shouldn't she be back by now? "Shit," he muttered, racing toward the storeroom.

He hit the swinging doors at a run. "Stacey," he yelled.

Brady and Cash hurried past the stacked pallets of beer and the giant cooler. Cash's lungs tightened and squeezed out his oxygen. The back door stood wide open. A body lay crumpled next to the dumpster. He heard Brady on the phone asking for an ambulance and the police.

Jonathan moaned and tried to sit up. A bloody rock lay next to him.

"Where is Stacey?" he asked.

Jonathan grabbed his head and collapsed on the ground. "I don't know."

"Take care of him." Cash left Brady bending over the wounded Jonathan.

Cash's gaze swept the parking area. He raced to the handful of pickups and cars, looking inside each of them. His pulse pounded in his ears. The vehicles were empty.

Hate boiled up from inside. He dialed Ash. He answered on the second ring.

"What have you learned about Simmons?"

"Not much. You just asked today," Ash groaned. "I did get his address and drive over. The apartment manager hasn't seen him for days. Something else happen?"

"Stacey's missing. Gone. Taken from under my fucking nose." Cash jerked his hat from his head. It seemed to be squeezing tighter and tighter. "I'll kill the son of a bitch."

"Take it easy. Only in self-defense or to save a life. Got it?"

"Yeah. Find out what Simmons drives. Call me with anything."

Chapter Eight

Cash stalked the parking lot like a caged animal. He and Detective Kelly had questions for Jonathan, but EMTs insisted they tended to him first.

"You're not talking to him without me," Cash growled when Kelly started toward the ambulance.

"No. I don't reckon I am." Kelly gave a resolved shrug. "Every squad car has been alerted. Anyone even swerves on the road and they'll be pulled over."

"Ray Simmons hasn't been seen in days. He has to be here in town." Cash had been in precarious situations before but it had been his own life at stake. This was Stacey and he didn't know which way to run. "Hell, you can't stop everyone. We don't even know what kind of vehicle we're looking for."

"How do you know this about Simmons? Never mind. It doesn't matter."

The lead EMT waved them over. "The rock hit at an odd angle, glanced off, and didn't do much damage. He doesn't have a concussion."

"Why all the blood?" Kelly asked.

"Almost all head injuries bleed like hell. You can talk to him."

Cash pulled his temper inside. He'd be no use to Stacey if he didn't maintain control. He beat Kelly to the back of the ambulance and heard Jonathan whine and insist he just wanted to go home.

"You were supposed to be watching her. What the hell happened?" Cash demanded.

"I don't know. She raised the lid on the dumpster for me to throw in the bags of trash, and the lights went out. I didn't see anything." Jonathan looked at Kelly who'd pushed himself in front. "Can I go now?"

"No," Kelly answered. "How the hell did this happen?"

"I just told Cash. I. Don't. Know. I'm sorry."

Cash wanted to shake him like a rag doll, if for nothing else whining like a girl.

"Go." Kelly intervened. "If you remember anything give me a call. You need somebody to follow you?"

"No. I'm good," Jonathan stood, proving his balance was fine by standing on one foot. He reached out to Cash's shoulder and patted. "I hope you find her."

Cash's cell vibrated. He stepped away to see what Ash had learned. "What have you got?"

"Simmons drives a red Explorer. Should be easy to spot."

His words stopped Cash in his tracks. His throat closed. Confusion crept in. Parked in the last slot behind the building sat the perfect match. He ran to the rear of the SUV and spit out the license plate number. "Does this one belong to Simmons?"

"Yeah. Did the Oak Hill cops finally come through?"

"No. I'm looking at his ride." Cash ended the call. He yelled for Kelly and started trying to open the doors. "This is Ray's car. There's a sleeping bag or quilt in the back. Dammit. No telling how long he'd been in town."

"What's the car doing here if he's got Stacey?"

"She rode with me, so they didn't leave in her car." Cash stepped closer to the Explorer. "Open it or I'll bust a window."

"No need for that. I've got probable cause." Kelly yelled for Bubba to bring the slim-jim and pop the door lock.

Bubba opened the door and looked inside. He stepped back fast. "I see a hand."

"Son of a bitch," Kelly climbed inside, unzipped the sleeping bag, and revealed a dead body underneath the sleeping bag.

"What the hell does this mean?" Cash's mind staggered. "If that's Ray, who took Stacey?"

Kelly tossed a few curse words out then rolled the body far enough to two-finger the wallet from his pocket. He closed his eyes after removing the driver's license.

"It's Simmons."

Cash spun around. Undecided about what to do next, he paced the parking lot. Time had become a commodity he couldn't waste. He moved back to the dumpster, looking for anything the cops might have missed. The cops had placed a yellow flag next to the rock used to knock out Jonathan. Cash replayed everything through his mind, eliminating possibilities one at a time. He stopped on the obvious. Damn.

Only one person could have taken her. "Kelly," Cash shouted.

He spun and scanned the crowd for Brady. Cash uttered a curse and sprinted to the building.

****

Stacey opened her eyes and tried to look around. Rockets explode inside her head. The sound of a car engine said she was inside someone's trunk. Her arms and ankles had been pulled behind her and lashed together with something so tightly it prevented her from kicking or pulling the emergency release.

Her joints protested being stretched into the unnatural pose. Stacey's shoulders were being ripped from their sockets with every bump of the road.

Moving brought waves of agony. She struggled to pull her jumbled thoughts together. She wanted to scream only her lips had been taped closed.

It had to be Ray. He'd waited for her behind the bar, which meant he'd watched her for a while. Could she talk her way out of this? Get free and defend herself? Other than the movies, she'd never even seen a fight. Didn't matter. She'd fight to survive. Adrenaline rushed through her, and she struggled to stay under control.

She remembered helping Jonathan carry out the trash. What had happened next? Her mind couldn't put the events together, but she had no doubt who'd taken her. Ray Simmons.

Panic welled inside her chest. She had to get help. Had to get away. But how? Trussed up like a roping steer at a rodeo, every movement brought mind-numbing pain.

Her thoughts turned to Cash. Beautiful, sexy, loving Cash. Their chance at happiness had been wrenched out of their hands. No. She would not have a defeatist attitude. She had to get back to him. She'd pretend to cooperate with Ray. Convince him that she'd come to her senses. At the first opportunity, she'd figure out how to escape.

The car stopped and idled for a minute. Her heart raced, pounding painfully against her ribs. She struggled to catch a calming breath. Was he having second thoughts? He'd threatened to cut her. Was he pulling a knife from his scabbard? Was he going to kill her right away? Her mind silently screamed.

The engine died, and the car shook when the door slammed home. The trunk latch popped, and a bright light shined in her eyes.

"Why won't you just stay dead? I won't let you hurt Jonathan ever again," the strange voice behind the light spoke. Stacey's confusion worsened. This wasn't Ray. It sounded as if her attacker was a woman.

The person dragged her face down from the trunk to the ground, ignoring her screams of pain. Suddenly, her hands and feet were freed. Laser hot pain flooded her limbs the second blood circulated through her deprived limbs. She worked her fingers under the tape on her mouth, pulling it loose and sucking in a deep breath.

"Get on your feet," the woman commanded.

With very little feeling in her hands and arms, Stacey managed to push herself up on all fours. Her kidnapper planted a foot against Stacey's butt and pushed, sending her sprawling, face first, across the dirt. An eerie giggle exploded from the stranger, filling the darkness with an insane echo.

"Why are you doing this?" Stacey brushed dirt from her mouth, rolling to face her attacker. "Where am I?

"Don't play dumb with me. We're home."

The person moved forward, grabbed her by the arm, and dragged her to her feet.

"Fun's over. I only cut you loose so you could walk inside. Now, go."

Her attacker was close enough for her to see. She blinked, refusing to believe her eyes. This wasn't a woman. Not at all. "Jonathan?"

He shrieked. The sound of a wild animal came from him. "Don't you dare say his name. Do it again, and I'll kill you here in the yard."

Even though the words had come from Jonathan, his voice had taken on a higher pitched, feminine sound. He wrapped a chunk of her hair around his hand, pressed the blade of a hunting knife to her throat, and pulled her toward a small house. Together they walked up the steps onto a rickety porch that squeaked from the pressure of each step. He shoved her inside.

Stumbling forward, she tried to reason with him. "Please, don't do something you'll regret."

"Shut up and sit down." He removed the bandana from his neck and tied her hands behind her back.

Lights flooded the room. Her friend Jonathan glared at her. But this wasn't the sweet young man she knew. He circled her chair. Hate and contempt filled his blue eyes, turning his lips into a snarl.

He backed off and then approached a couple of times. He'd lean close to her face and then look away. He'd morphed into a total stranger. A madman.

"I should've known better than to try to scare you off. Someone as evil as you won't go away. You are supposed to be dead." His eyebrows pulled together. "So why do I have to kill you over and over?"

"I don't understand. What do you think I did, Jona—" The blow knocked her out of the chair. She lay sprawled on the floor while the acrid taste of blood filled her mouth.

He grabbed her hair again and dragged her back onto the chair. But not before she noticed the knot in the bandana had loosened. Her hands were still behind her back but not behind the chair. She fought to remain calm and to work her hands-free.

He smoothed his disheveled hair, straightened his shirt, and then slammed one hand on his hip. He glared at her with an indignant expression.

Bile flooded the back of Stacey's throat. His mannerisms—his way of standing—and his voice, Jonathan had taken on a feminine persona.

"Don't talk to me like I'm stupid," he said in a high-pitched voice, baring his teeth. Snarling, he looked like a wolf about to attack. "I know all the horrible things you did to him. I heard his screams. Don't pretend you don't deserve what's coming."

Tears stung Stacey's eyes, but she battled them back. Jonathan's personality had fractured. Split. Who had control of his mind? Maybe if she went along with him, stalled him, she'd buy enough time to free herself. She caught his gaze and held, fighting not to flinch.

"I don't think you're stupid," she said, working hard to keep her voice calm.

"No, I'm not. Neither is he," Jonathan said, advancing, waving the knife. "But he's much easier to manipulate than me. You tried to convince him he was evil, but I saved him. Saved him from you."

"He's not evil. He's my friend." Her heart bled for the sweet young man she'd worked with because he'd gone completely mad. "Just like Lance was."

Jonathan swung and the blade sliced through the sleeve of her blouse, grazing her arm. A burning sensation followed and blood seeped through the thin cotton material.

"Don't you blame me for that. I didn't kill him. Your stalker murdered your stalker." He giggled. "Get it? Lance followed you around at work, and the other guy followed you home from the bar. Him, I killed." Jonathan huffed out a sound of disgust. "You should thank me."

"So Ray *was* here." Stacey's blood chilled. It hadn't been her imagination; he had been following her.

"Yes." His shrill voice raised another octave. "You'll see him soon. In hell."

He flicked the tip of the blade through the denim in her jeans. The surface cut stung, and she cried out. Staying under control got harder by the minute. She had to keep him talking. One more pull and her hands would be free.

"You're bleeding," she asked "Are you hurt?"

"No. I hit Jonathan with a rock. Everybody believed your stalker knocked him out." His smile sent shivers down Stacey's back. "So if you're waiting to be rescued, you can forget that."

He took a step closer. When he moved into range, Stacey drew back both feet and kicked. The blow caught him off guard and knocked him to the floor. The knife skittered across the carpet, with Stacey scrambling on her hands and knees to grab it.

The handle was less than an inch away. One last stretch and she'd have the knife.

Jonathan grabbed her hair, yanked her back, and slung her to the side.

Her head bounced off the hard floor. An array of stars detonated behind her eyes. He rolled her over, straddling her. Stacey caught his wrists in her hands to hold him off, but the blade descended and sunk deep into her chest, slicing through tendons and muscles.

"Die!" He pulled the knife out and raised it high over his head.

She lifted her hips and kicked her feet to unseat him.

The front door exploded. He whirled around, relaxing his attention on her. That gave her the chance she needed to knock him off balance. Jonathan tumbled off her.

Rushing toward her, Cash's eyes were stone cold. Jonathan's eyes flashed wild and wide. The burning pain in her chest didn't keep Stacey from scooting backward and out of the way. A burst of crimson covered her blouse. Damn, there was too much blood. Even the waistband of her jeans was wet. Had he hit an artery?

A loud shriek exploded from Jonathan. The sound was like something from a horror movie. With the knife held high in the air, he rushed Cash.

The fight was over before it started. Through the fog forming in front of her eyes, she watched Cash deftly block the oncoming blow and slam his fist into Jonathan's face. The crack of the bone breaking in Jonathan's jaw filled the room.

Cash rushed to her. He ripped off his shirt, gathered her in his arms, and pressed the cloth against her wound. From somewhere in the background, she heard Detective Kelly on his radio ordering additional backup and an ambulance.

"Please don't leave me," Cash whispered.

She tried to smile, tried to offer assurance, but what she wanted was to sleep.

****

Stacey shifted and a stab of pain in her right shoulder snapped her from drowsy to wide awake. The stark white walls matched the color of the bandage peeking out from under her cotton hospital gown. She wiggled her fingers and then flexed her hand. Everything worked.

Next to her bed, slumped down in a chair with his long legs stretched out in front of him, Cash snored lightly. Dark lashes cast shadows over the circles under his sleeping eyes. Judging from the stubble on his chin, she hadn't been out long.

She ached to reach out to him. To touch him. Hold him. To thank him. But she didn't have the heart to wake him. Instead, she lay in silence until his eyelids fluttered and opened to small slits. Her body warmed when that lazy, sexy smile slid across his face.

"Hello, beautiful," she said.

"Men aren't beautiful," he reminded her, pushing himself upright.

"Mine is."

"You scared the shit out of me."

"Scared me too. I won't do it again."

"See to it that you don't." He rose, leaned over, and kissed her forehead.

"That the best you can do?"

"For now."

"Jonathan?"

"In the county mental ward. Kelly dug up some pretty scary shit. Jonathan thought you were his grandmother. She believed all men were evil. When her unmarried daughter died giving birth, she blamed Jonathan. Tortured him for years before he ran away."

"He came home when she died. Wonder if that's when his personality split."

"I'm not an expert on that stuff, but I'm guessing the alter ego took over a long time ago when the torture became too much for him to take. Maybe being back in her house was the catalyst for his break with reality. Unless he starts talking, no one may ever know everything that happened in that house."

"Somewhere he and Ray crossed paths." She repeated Jonathan's confessions. The two men had been on a collision course, and Ray lost the race. "So we don't know who killed my landlady."

Cash shifted his weight, there was more he hadn't said. Funny how she was learning to read those stormy eyes. "What aren't you telling me?"

"A search of Jonathan's place revealed three brushes. Kelly's waiting on DNA results on the hair, but he believes one is yours and the others belonged to two murdered women he's been investigating."

"That's why Jonathan said I wouldn't stay dead. I should tell Kelly."

"He'll be here later today. No doubt, he'll be full of questions." Cash walked to the doorway and looked down the hall.

"There's more you're not saying."

He turned and took a deep breath. "Your dad will be here soon."

The muscles in her neck and shoulders bunch. "Who called him?"

"I got his number off your throwaway and called him. He'd have seen it on the news anyway. Nothing would be accomplished by scaring the crap out of him."

"I'm not sure I want to see him. He hurt both of us." Her heart melted that Cash had taken what had to be a difficult step toward forgiving her dad. "He's never going to change. Know this, if he tries to force me to choose, you will always win."

"I don't doubt that. Sometimes it's best to leave the past in the past. The whole thing sounds foolish now. You and I will start fresh. Build a life and family with or without your daddy's approval."

"But I'll never forgive how badly he treated your mother."

A wistful smile lifted the corner of his mouth. "She'd be the first to tell us to let it go. I almost lost you. Again. Life is too damn short for me to stay pissed at your father."

In a couple of long strides, Cash was next to her. He held out his hand. "As long as we love each other, we don't need anyone else's approval."

"Do we have each other? I do need someone to watch over me." She twined her fingers through his, looked deep into his stormy eyes, and saw trust. The warm undercurrent in his gaze confirmed it.

"Damn right, we have each other." In a couple of long strides, he leaned over her. "I'm here forever?"

"Yes, forever." She ignored the pain and pulled him down for a kiss. Actions were much better than words.

About the Author

A student of creative writing in her youth, Jerrie set aside her passion when life presented her with a John Wayne husband and a wonderful daughter. Her love for romantic suspense inspires her to write alpha males and kick-ass women. Her characters weave their way through death and danger to emerge stronger, because of, and on occasion, in spite of, their love for each other. If they're tough enough, they live happily ever after.

Jerrie lives in Texas, denies having an accent, thrives on sunshine, children's laughter, sugar (human and granulated), and researching for her heroes and heroines. She loves to hear from her readers. Find a complete list of her books at http://www.jerriealexander.com or contact her at jerrie@jerriealexander.com.

Read more at www.jerriealexander.com.